The Lady at 99

ENID GIBSON

The Lady at 99

DRAGON

Dragon Books
Granada Publishing Ltd
8 Grafton Street, London W1X 3LA

Published by Dragon Books 1985

British Library Cataloguing in Publication Data

Gibson, Enid
  The Lady at 99.
  I. Title
  823'.914[J]   PZ7

ISBN 0-583-30694-2

Printed and bound in Great Britain by
Collins, Glasgow

Set in Times

Chapter 1

'Wake up, Pet. We're almost there.'

Emma Morris heard her father's voice through restless dreams and forced open her heavy eyelids. The windscreen wipers were still beating their monotonous rhythm, but the car was heading out of the rainswept Downs and descending a steep, winding hill.

'You can just see Athelbury now,' said Mr Morris. 'Lovely town. You'll like it there.'

Turning her head, Emma peered out across lush green fields to a distant, mist-shrouded hill. A tall church spire dominated the skyline. Grey rooftops, clustering about it, were barely glimpsed before low, drifting clouds obscured the view, leaving her unimpressed. Having no inkling of the horror awaiting her there, she yawned sleepily and settled back in her seat once more. No doubt Athelbury was pretty enough on a fine day, she thought, but in weather like this it seemed remote and dismal.

The heavy rain had eased to a light drizzle by the time they were cruising up the narrow and hilly High Street, in search of Aunt Peggy's house. The street was deserted, save for a few of the faithful making their way to church for the Sunday evening service.

Halfway up the hill, Mr Morris brought the car to rest outside a shop with a dark blind pulled down inside the large window. Faded lettering across the doorway read, 'Travis Groceries'.

'Well, Pet. This is it.' Mr Morris sounded weary as he stepped from the car, opened the boot and took out a blue leather suitcase.

Emma stood on the pavement and gazed about her cheerlessly, realizing that her cotton skirt had creased badly. If only her father had let her wear jeans, but he had insisted on a skirt and blouse, just as he had insisted on bringing his daughter to Dorset when her mother had been taken ill.

'But it's nonsense, Dad,' Emma had protested. 'I'll be thirteen next Tuesday. I'm quite capable of running the house while Mum's in hospital.'

But her father had been obdurate. 'Had you been at school, I wouldn't have worried so much, but with three weeks of holidays left I'd rather know you were safe with adults while I'm at work.'

So it was that Emma now found herself succumbing to the warm and buxom embrace of a plump, motherly woman who had come to the door to greet them.

'My, Emma! Let me look at you.' Aunt Peggy beamed down at the grey eyes peeping out from beneath a thick blonde fringe. 'How you've grown! Yet your hair is still like spun gold. You are a lucky creature to have that.'

Instinctively, Emma shook her long straight mane and wished she could remember this aunt whose cheerful manner made her spirits lift a little, but all she now knew of this family was that her Uncle Gerry had died four years ago, leaving his wife, two children and a small grocery shop. Her cousins, she thought, must be in their early teens; and a wave of apprehension swept over her at the thought of meeting them. She hated meeting strangers and was always tongue-tied, but this time would be even worse since, like them or hate them, she would have to live with Becky and Mark for at least two weeks.

Aunt Peggy bustled about Emma and her father, talking the while. 'You must be worn out, you poor dears. Tea's ready, but come upstairs with me first, Emma, and I'll show you your room. You go on into the sitting room, Bill. You remember where it is, just one flight up.'

As they turned to follow her across the darkened shop, Emma almost collided with a thick oak pillar which rose from floor to ceiling. She wondered if it held up the ancient building and speculated about what might happen if death watch beetle ate right through it. Musty age mingled with the smells of yesterday's cheese and fruit; timber beams seemed strangely at odds with the modern glass counter and white plastic trays set within it, while more incongruous still was the deep freeze unit by the far wall.

Aunt Peggy was breathless by the time she had climbed the two steep flights to the bedrooms. 'I've put you in the front, dear,' she puffed. 'It used to be Becky's room but she found it too noisy with all the traffic, so I changed her to the back. I do hope you'll sleep alright, though. Still, I daresay you're used to noise, coming from London.'

Emma smiled, for all it seemed odd that life in the country would prove to be more noisy than her tree-lined avenue in Croydon. 'It's lovely, Aunty. I'll sleep like a log, don't worry.'

7

Right now, she could have slept on a clothes line in a storm, for the past three days had been filled with worry and tension. Only when it became clear that her mother's sudden illness would not be fatal did she and her father relax a little, but the long hours of driving through rain today had left them both fraying at the edges and desperate for rest. She put her case on to the bed and cast her eyes round the shell-pink walls and pretty flowered curtains. The floors were uneven, indeed the whole house seemed to be tilted, and it felt strange to walk downhill towards the dressing table.

Her first meeting with Becky, however, was to be an uphill encounter.

Aunt Peggy had arranged high tea for her guests, and while she and her brother had plenty to talk about, Emma found herself seated opposite Becky who just stared across the table in hostile silence.

Six months older than Emma, and a striking-looking girl with sleek dark hair cut close to her head, Becky's green eyes were cold and regarded her cousin with watchful suspicion, making it all too obvious that Emma was unwelcome.

Emma toyed with her chicken salad, trying not to meet those unfriendly eyes; but whatever she did, wherever she looked, she could feel them boring into her until she wanted to scream out, 'Stop it, stop it at once! I'll leave this very minute if that's what you want.' She felt utterly wretched and hoped Mark would prove more approachable than his younger sister; but he had not put in an appearance and no one had mentioned him, save for the usual polite enquiries made by her father.

As the meal progressed the feeling of wretchedness gave way to something deeper, and a strange sense of foreboding swept over Emma. She told herself it was tiredness, combined with Becky's attitude, but still it persisted, growing with each moment until she shuddered.

'Would you like a cardigan, dear?' asked Aunt Peggy. 'You seem cold.'

Emma looked up, startled by the sudden question. The spell was broken and the foreboding swept away.

"Er . . . no. No, thank you. I'm fine, really I am.'

The rumble of a passing lorry woke Emma. She lay still for a while, staring at the unfamiliar surroundings and wondering where she was, but as memory returned she slipped out of bed, put on her blue cotton dressing gown and pushed up the window. At once the noise of traffic and hurried footsteps met her ears.

She leaned out and looked down on Athelbury's narrow High Street. Even at this hour the August sun was warm, soaking up the water from yesterday's rain and striking full on to the fruit and vegetables stacked in boxes outside the greengrocer's shop directly opposite. A man came out of the building carrying a pole which he used to pull down a green awning to protect his produce from the hot day ahead.

She looked uphill towards the Market Square. On the far side stood a large white building with 'Bear Hotel' written across the wall in black lettering. But the square was dominated by the ornately-built

Town Hall. It stood hard by the ancient stone church, and was turreted, which gave it a fairy tale look. The clock on its high tower chimed the half hour.

Emma looked at her watch. It was half past eight. Glancing down quickly, she saw that her father's car was still parked there and sighed with relief. Not that he would have left her here without saying goodbye; but nevertheless, it was good to be certain.

Wondering what this day would bring, she dressed quickly in clean jeans and a red checked overshirt, then walked down narrow winding stairs to the small dining room. Mr Morris was seated at the table, reading a newspaper and drinking coffee. He put down the cup and paper, then kissed his daughter.

'Did you sleep well, Pet?'

'Like a log. How about you?'

'Dead to the world.' He finished his coffee and stood up. 'But I must be off now. I'm just waiting for your aunt.'

'Where is she?'

'In the shop.'

'Already?'

Mr Morris took off his glasses and smiled. 'There's more to running a shop than just opening up on time. Your aunt's a busy lady, which is why we never get to see each other these days. I daresay she'd welcome a helping hand.'

'Yes, I'll help, if she wants me to.'

An awkward pause followed, and Emma hovered beside her father wondering how he would react if she asked him to take her home again. It was unthinkable, however, and now the farewells must be said. At a time such as this, they were especially painful to both father and daughter.

Aunt Peggy entered at that moment and Mr Morris patted his side pockets in the way he always did when feeling embarrassed.

'Well then. Er . . . well then, I'd best be making tracks, I suppose.' He turned to his daughter. 'Now don't you worry about your mother, Pet, she'll be fine. The doctors are very hopeful.'

'You'll phone me?' Emma felt a painful lump form in her throat.

'Every night, just as soon as I return from the hospital. That's a firm promise.' Mr Morris bent and kissed his daughter. 'Now you're not to worry. Enjoy your birthday tomorrow. We'll celebrate it when your mother's home again.'

At length, when the goodbyes had been said, Emma stood on the pavement and watched the car drive up the High Street and across the Market Square until it disappeared out of sight.

'How would you like to help me in the shop this morning?'

She felt the motherly arm about her shoulders and fought back stinging tears. All she could do was nod in answer to her aunt's suggestion. Being busy would take her mind off things, and help to right the world which, for Emma, had suddenly spun off its axis.

She wondered where her cousins were and why neither of them had bothered to get up to say goodbye to her father. Mark she had still not met, since he came in long after she had gone to bed last night, but Becky had met both Emma and her father. For her, there was no excuse. Emma bristled with anger at the thought. Who was it said that good manners was only a matter of putting others at their ease? Clearly Becky Travis had no intention of doing any such thing, and who could say what Mark would be like?

She turned and followed her aunt into the shop where she watched her slicing ham on the machine at the back of the counter, then placing it in the plastic trays next to the bacon and cheese. Aunt Peggy paused as a black Labrador came trotting in from the back of the shop.

'Out, Sheba! Out at once.'

The bitch looked up at her with soft brown eyes, grumbled, then turned and trotted out again.

'She tries it on from time to time,' laughed Aunt Peggy. 'But you have to be very firm. I don't mind where she goes in the flat, but she's not allowed in the shop at all. No dogs are.'

The morning passed quickly enough since Emma spent most of it unpacking boxes of jam and marmalade, setting them out on shelves then taking the empty cartons into the yard. From time to time she wondered if her cousins ever helped their mother, and was deeply hurt when she caught a glimpse of Becky slipping out quietly through the back door. Thank goodness for her aunt and Sheba, she thought, otherwise life in Athelbury would have been intolerable. Resolving never to put anyone through the misery Becky was putting her through, Emma turned her attention to the elderly woman who had been chatting to Aunt Peggy and was now having great difficulty at the counter.

'Thank you, my dear,' murmured Mrs Percy as

Emma put her purchases into the large shopping bag on wheels. 'Your aunt tells me you'll be thirteen tomorrow.'

Emma watched the wrinkled hands shake as the fingers fumbled in a purse for money, and noticed how the trembling chin had a large mole from which grew two whiskery hairs. Mrs Percy looked very old, she thought; so old, in fact, that a puff of wind might blow her away.

'You don't look thirteen, my dear.'

Emma was used to this because of her small stature. She knew the next line by heart also.

'And you're very pale.' Mrs Percy peered at her with deep concern. 'She's very pale, Mrs Travis. Is she ill?'

Aunt Peggy smiled. 'She comes from London. Never mind, a few windy days on this hill should put some colour in those cheeks.'

'It's all this television,' said Mrs Percy. 'They watch far too much television when they should be outside.' She handed Emma a coin. 'It's only fifty pence. I know it's not much these days. But buy yourself some sweets or something for your birthday tomorrow, and many happy returns, my dear.'

When she had gone, Emma turned to her aunt who had climbed on the footstool to reach the upper shelves. 'I didn't like to take it really, but she might have been offended.'

'Oh, she would have been.'

At that moment the shop bell clanged loudly, as it always did when someone left or entered the store. Both aunt and niece turned, expecting to see a customer, but no one had entered.

13

'Strange,' murmured Aunt Peggy. 'I didn't see anyone in here just now, did you?'

'There wasn't anyone. Not unless they were hidden by the pillar.'

'Even so. Why walk out without being served?' Aunt Peggy was clearly perturbed. 'Oh dear, I do hope I haven't offended anyone, by seeming to ignore them.'

Emma sensed her anxiety, for the thought had already occurred to her that this little shop did not do a roaring business. In spite of the fact that Monday trade was always light, she had noticed that the grocery store across the road seemed to attract most of the morning's shoppers.

Becky appeared at lunch time, when she minced into the dining room in jeans and white sweat shirt, then took her place without a word to Emma.

'Where's Mark?' sighed Aunt Peggy.

Becky shrugged. 'Gone to Graham's, I expect.'

'Well, he might have said hello to Emma first.' Aunt Peggy was clearly angry. 'I especially asked him to make an effort. It's too bad of him, truly it is. Youngsters have no manners these days. It's not as though I didn't teach you any.'

'Well, don't blame me,' said Becky. 'I'm not my brother's keeper.'

Over a lunch of cheese, pickles and French bread, Aunt Peggy gave firm orders that Emma was to get out into the sun. 'Becky will show you around.'

Banished into the hot August sunshine and the uncomfortable company of each other, the girls walked slowly along the garden path amidst a blaze of colour. Dahlias, astors and fuchsia grew in healthy

14

abundance, ending by a stone wall. The wall was low, and beyond it the ridge fell away to a large vale where stone farms dotted the fields as they stretched far into the distant blue hills of Somerset.

The view was breathtaking and made Emma forget the angry silence between them. She turned to her cousin, smiling.

'It's beautiful. I didn't realize Athelbury was so high.'

Becky watched her but said nothing, then folded her arms and contemplated her sandals in a sullen fashion until Emma's exasperated question disarmed her.

'What is it? Why do I upset you so much, for goodness sake?'

'I don't know what you mean.'

Deciding anger would get her nowhere, Emma took a deep breath and tried to calm down.

'Alright, so you don't like my being here. But it's only for a week or so. Have I taken your bedroom? Is that it? Your mother said you preferred the back because it was quieter.'

'It has nothing to do with the bedroom.' Becky's voice had the merest hint of a Dorset accent.

'What then?'

Becky turned from her cousin, walked towards the wall, then sat down upon it. For a long time she just stared out at the vale, then finally she murmured, 'I wish you hadn't come here.'

'I can see that, but why?'

'Because your being here frightens me.'

This was the last thing Emma had expected her cousin to say, and she could only stare at her in amazement. At last she managed to find her voice.

'Why do I frighten you?'

'*You* don't. It's . . . well, it's the darkness all about you that frightens me. I was warned of it. Warned of fear and danger coming with the stranger who brings the darkness.'

Emma frowned. 'What are you talking about? What darkness?'

'She said a stranger would come, bringing fear, danger and darkness. And here you are. Just as she foretold. She must have meant you. There's no one else.'

Emma felt no alarm at this, just confusion and a growing suspicion that her cousin was playing some silly joke on her. Yet closer inspection of those frightened eyes dispelled the suspicion quickly, leaving only bewilderment.

'Who told you this?'

'Mary Ann.'

'A friend of yours?'

Becky nodded and glanced at her cousin from beneath hooded lids. 'A woman who grows herbs for the shop. A friend.

'She sounds very odd.'

'She's a seer.'

'A what?'

Becky jumped from the wall and bent to stroke Sheba who had come trotting down the garden to join them. 'She sees into the future.'

'How?'

'By reading tea-leaves.'

'Oh, that!'

Emma was unimpressed, and quite relieved. Her mother's friend read the leaves and came to hysterical conclusions which, thankfully, never materialized into fact. It was just fun. Becky, however, was clearly a deeply superstitious girl, and a willing audience for some cranky woman who basked in her girlish admiration so that the fun became all too serious.

'And you believe her?' Emma could not help but smile.

'Of course,' said Becky. 'After all, she told me about this last Tuesday. And here you are. Who else could she have meant?'

Emma stopped smiling and frowned. Her mother had been taken ill in the supermarket on Thursday morning, and not until Friday evening had her father decided she would have to come here. Yet Becky had been told of it on Tuesday?

'It's a coincidence, that's all.'

Becky shook her dark head slowly from side to side. 'Mary Ann is never wrong. She really does have the power to see things.'

'No one has that power.'

'Mary Ann has it.

Emma sniffed with an air of contempt, but felt a shade more perturbed than before. Nevertheless, she was too level-headed to give Mary Ann more importance than she deserved.

'I think she's got a cheek, talking about me like that. Fear, danger and darkness, did you say? Rubbish! She just enjoys frightening you, and now you're trying to frighten me. She's no more able to foretell the future than I am.'

Becky was staring down into the vale once more, and Emma followed her frightened eyes to an untidy

17

spread of modern caravans, partly hidden by a clump of trees. A thin spiral of smoke drifted upwards from an unseen fire, and a baby's cry disturbed the still air.

'The gipsies are back in Swallow Field.' Becky almost hissed the words, spitting them out like drops of cold water striking hot metal.

Emma looked at her cousin's taut mouth, wondering why she was so alarmed. 'There's no harm in gipsies.'

Becky stared at her in surprise. 'If you lived here, you wouldn't say that. Still, you being from London, you won't know about them.'

'Why? *Now* what's the matter?'

'*They're* what's the matter,' said Becky pointing.

Emma laughed. 'Oh come on, now! What harm can they do?'

'They do great harm.'

'Such as?'

'Mary Ann could tell you a thing or two about them. They took a girl once; took her away, and she's never been seen again.'

Emma looked surprised. 'Oh. What happened?'

Becky shrugged. 'No one knows. It happened a long time ago. But folk hereabouts have never forgotten, or forgiven.'

'What makes you think the gipsies had anything to do with it?'

'It's common knowledge.' Becky shrugged. 'Of course the gipsies denied it. Well, they would, wouldn't they? But it's true, just the same.' She paused and stared hard at Emma, with the realization that her cousin doubted her. 'Alright!' she cried out angrily. 'Believe what you like, but Mary Ann will tell you. She knew the girl.'

Emma watched her cousin walk back along the garden path, and felt her heart sink with despair. This Mary Ann had a great deal to answer for, in her opinion. What a pity it was that she could not spend her birthday with her own intelligent friends, instead of this morose and superstitious girl who seemed intent upon frightening her.

That evening Emma saw Mark for the first time. He burst into the sitting room, nodded briefly to her, murmured something about the chain coming off his bike, and went out as quickly as he had entered, leaving her with the memory of some tall, dishevelled youth with medium length blond hair, oil covered jeans and a blue denim jacket. She wondered who fed him, since he was never around at meal times, and likened him in her mind to a wild cat who used to come to their back door when desperation drove him there.

It was Sheba who made her feel wanted that evening. While Aunt Peggy worked on her accounts and Becky sat watching the television, the bitch leaned up against Emma's legs, looking at her with loving brown eyes as she fondled the black silky ears. She had always wanted a dog, but her parents had been set against it. 'Animals are such a tie,' they would say. 'Who would look after it if we wanted to go away for the weekend?' But they hardly ever went away at weekends and Emma had stopped asking long ago.

At nine o'clock Mr Morris phoned through to say that her mother was out of danger now, and that the doctors were happier about her condition. He wished Emma a happy birthday, and hoped she would like the present he had left with her aunt.

So it was that, after a good night's rest, Emma came down to breakfast the following morning to find cards and three packages beside her plate. Aunt Peggy had taken some trouble with the table, bringing out her best chinaware and placing freshly-cut roses in the centre to set off the lace table-cloth. But more astonishing still was the sight of Mark and Becky seated in their places already. She found herself wondering what threats her aunt had uttered to get them up so early for this day.

'Happy birthday, Emma,' said Mark cheerfully.

'Happy birthday,' murmured Becky.

Emma thanked them both for their greeting, their card and their large box of chocolates, all of which were a very great surprise. Then her eyes were drawn to the silver package decorated with a pink satin bow. It was from her parents. Excitedly, she unwrapped the paper and took out the hair-dryer she had wanted for so long, remembering the day, in Croydon, when she and her mother had eyed the various models in the shops. Tears stung her eyes suddenly.

Quick as a flash, Mark was on his feet and drawing her attention to another package, surprising Emma by his thoughtfulness. The gift was from Aunt Peggy and proved to be a silver chain and pendant.

'I didn't expect . . . I mean . . . well, thank you all.' Emma stammered the words, as they tumbled out with a mixture of emotions.

They had just finished their breakfast of eggs and bacon, and Aunt Peggy had barely opened the shop, when the bell clanged loudly.

'I'll go,' said Mark. 'Stay here, Mum, and finish your coffee.'

He returned almost at once with puzzlement on his face and a package in his hand. It was a book bound with crimson ribbon.

'The shop was empty,' he murmured, 'but this was on the counter. No note or anything. It must be for you, Em.'

Emma shook her head. 'It can't be. No one knows it's my birthday. No one knows me, full stop.'

Aunt Peggy put down her coffee cup and took the book. 'Well, now isn't that odd. Fancy leaving it on the counter and then rushing out again. I daresay it is for you though, dear. Here, you take it.'

Emma smiled, took the book and untied the wide ribbon. 'It smells musty,' she murmured gazing at the dark blue cover and the faded picture of three young women sitting under a tree. They were dressed in Edwardian clothes and the lettering, *The Girlhood of Sarah*, was ornately written in gold. She turned the cover and on the fly-leaf, tinged yellow with age, saw an inscription scrawled in black ink by a shaky hand: 'To Emma. Best wishes, from the lady at 99'.

'It's from the lady at ninety-nine.' Emma looked at her aunt. 'Is that Mrs Percy?'

Aunt Peggy looked puzzled and shook her head. 'No, she's at Cook's Lane. Ninety-nine has to be in the High Street. Now, let me see. The Gregsons are at seventy-four, and Ben's at ninety-eight, but then he doesn't know you anyway, and Mrs Beamish is at eighty-six, I think.' At last she gave up. 'No, I can't think who it could be. Now why on earth didn't she put her name?'

Becky took the book and winkled her nose in disgust. 'It smells old, damp even. Ugh, what a weird thing to give as a present.'

'That's not a nice thing to say,' said her mother disapprovingly. 'It *is* old, and was probably a cherished possession, so that makes it an extraordinary and generous gift.'

'But who can it be from?' asked Emma. 'No one else but Mrs Percy knows it's my birthday.' As she spoke, she remembered again the sound of the shop bell when the unseen customer had left yesterday. That was just after they had discussed her birthday with the old lady. She felt chilled suddenly, and realized that her aunt was talking to her.

'Wake up, dear. I was just saying that if you want to thank her you could write a note and pop it into her door today.'

'Yes. Yes, I could do that.'

'Shouldn't bother,' sniffed Becky.

'But I must,' said Emma.

'Of course you must.' Aunt Peggy glanced angrily at her daughter.

'But where is number ninety-nine?' Emma was turning the pages of the book.

'Somewhere in the High Street. It'll be the top end – across the Market Square. You'll find it.'

'It has to be the High Street,' said Mark, by way of explanation, 'Since it's the only road long enough to have a number ninety-nine. Anyway, good hunting.'

Emma put the book down on the table and nodded. 'Very well. I'll write a thank you note and put it in her letter box this afternoon.'

Chapter 2

The Town Hall clock was just striking three as Emma made her way along the High Street. It was still very hot and fumes from the traffic hung heavily on the oppressive air, so she walked slowly, taking time to glance into shop windows as she passed by.

The Market Square was empty of people and stalls, but several cars were parked outside the Bear Hotel. Emma stood beside them wondering where the High Street went to at this point. At length, she picked it up again and found herself walking along the outer edge of the town, past the cricket ground and into a narrow lane that twisted down steeply into the vale.

There were no shops now, just old stone cottages that fronted on to the pavement. Pausing at each one, Emma searched for a number, hoping to avoid having to walk too far down the hill on such a hot day.

'Sixty-eight, seventy, seventy-two.' Her heart sank. Ninety-nine would surely be at the bottom, especially as the cottages were becoming more spaced out.

She slowed her pace when she saw two gipsy women walking up the hill towards her. They each carried a wicker basket filled with bristling purple heather and, seeing Emma, moved directly into her path. The taller of the two women held out a bunch of heather.

'You've got a lucky face, my dear,' she murmured in a deep throaty voice. 'Buy some heather, for good fortune.'

Emma backed nervously into a wall, staring at the dank black hair and dark, shrewd eyes that were deeply etched into an olive skinned face, and smiled apologetically.

'I haven't any money, I'm afraid.'

The woman withdrew her hand, then flashed a broad and toothy grin.

'God bless you then, my dear.'

The other woman came forward, unsmiling. She was older than her companion and a red scarf covered her greying hair.

'Have a care, child.' she murmured, taking Emma by the arm. 'Have a care.'

With that she moved away suddenly and together the two women walked on, leaving Emma shaken and unnerved by the sudden encounter.

At a bend in the road she found herself looking across the great vale, with field after field reaching to the far distant, haze-shrouded hills. The only sound to be heard came from a lawn-mower somewhere down the hill; otherwise, it seemed that all England was sleeping.

Hot and sticky, Emma finally came to number ninety-seven and looked eagerly for its neighbour, but it was much further on and set well back from the road. As she approached, she saw how dilapidated and uncared for the stone cottage seemed. The thatched roof had fallen away in parts; the front door was rotten, with green paint flaking from it; no curtains hung at the dirty windows; nettles and briars had overtaken the garden, and the wooden gate was hanging off its hinges.

Confused, Emma stood staring for a long time, then turned her attention to the cottage opposite. This was well kept and covered with blue wisteria. Three apple trees guarded the neat front lawn, where an elderly man was pushing a hand mower. He caught sight of her shy approach and paused.

'Afternoon.'

'Good afternoon. Is this number ninety-nine?'

The man shook his bald head. 'No, m'dear. This is Wisteria Cottage. That's ninety-nine, over there.'

Emma looked to where he pointed and frowned. 'Oh. It seems empty.'

'That's right.'

'But I don't understand. The lady who lives there sent me a birthday present this morning. Do you know where she is?'

The man chuckled, took out a green handkerchief and mopped his sweating brow. 'Oh, I know that alright. She's in the churchyard. Has been these past four-and-twenty years or so.'

'Dead?' Emma's expression of consternation and disbelief surprised the man. 'Are you saying she's dead?'

'Well now, she's hardly likely to stay there otherwise, is she.' He stopped smiling and became curious. 'What's all this about a present?'

As Emma told him she saw his shoulders shake with mirth. 'I know the old girl is said to haunt,' he

25

said, 'but I've never heard of her sending gifts to people since she died.'

'She haunts?'

'That's right, or so I've been told.' He smiled knowingly. 'Someone's been having you on, I'd say. Didn't you know about Mrs Bennett, then? I thought everyone did.'

Emma felt anger rising within her. Of course it had been a joke. And who else would think of it but that Becky with her tales of woe and supernatural portents. She turned and stared at the cottage thoughtfully.

'Is that why it's empty? Because it's supposed to be haunted?'

The man nodded. 'Sad it is, and a disgrace, to see a fine old place like that go to ruin. She did have a son, but he lives in Australia. The place belongs to him now, and he won't sell it. He put tenants in once, but they were out within the week claiming they had seen things.'

'What things?'

The man smiled. 'A white haired old lady, clad all in black, walking through the walls. She's been seen in the garden, too, from time to time.'

He was teasing her, thought Emma, so she just laughed. 'But you've never seen anything?'

'Of course not. It's all a lot of nonsense, if you ask me. Some folk have too much imagination, that's all.' He looked across at the cottage thoughtfully, his eyes taking on a far away look as past images crowded his mind.

'Strange though, about the black dress. You see, Mrs Bennett always wore black, ever since her husband died during the First World War. She never came out of mourning for him. It made her seem older, somehow.'

'Did you know her?'

'Oh, aye. Kept herself to herself and wouldn't have help from anyone, but I saw her from time to time. Nice old thing. Gentle and kind. Loved children. There were always kiddies going in and out.' A shadow passed over his lined face. 'I think that's what killed her. Not old age, but heartbreak over that poor girl.'

'Which girl?'

'The one that disappeared.'

Emma frowned and remembered Becky's words: 'They took a girl once.' She hesitated before she spoke. 'I was told that the gipsies stole her away. Is it true?'

'No one knows what happened.' The man scratched his chin. 'It's been years and years. Even so, it seems like only yesterday to me. Come to think of it, this lass was like you to look at; smallish, pretty, and with long fair hair. How old are you?'

'Thirteen.' It seemed strange, saying it aloud.

'Mmm, she'd be about that age, too. I blame myself, I do. I blame myself for not staying in the garden that Saturday . . .' His voice trailed off. 'But there we are. Wise after the event, as ever. I'd often seen her at the cottage but this time she carried some flowers. I was weeding at the time. It was a perfect summer's day. Suddenly, I heard shouts and saw this other smaller girl, running towards her. The two started quarrelling dreadfully so I went back into the house for some peace and quiet. The next thing I knew I was staring at her picture in the newspaper. Disappeared, she had. The police were searching high and low for her. They'd even dragged the river at Nettlemarsh.' He paused and bit his bottom lip. 'I daresay I was the last person to see the girl. Mrs Bennett was dreadfully upset. She never got over it, poor old soul, and died three weeks later. Grief it was, I'm quite sure of it.'

'And the girl was never found, alive or dead?'

The man shook his head, then brightened. 'But if you don't know all this, you'd not be from these parts then.'

'No, I'm from Croydon. I'm staying with my aunt, Mrs Travis. She has a shop in the . . .'

'Peggy! Well, well, so you're Peggy's niece. You tell her you saw Ben now, Ben Palmer. Give her my regards. Tell her Gladys is much better – that's my wife – and tell her I'll be in on Friday, as usual.'

Emma turned and, as she did so, happened to glance once more at the cottage. She stiffened. 'There's someone in there. I – I thought I saw someone at the window.'

Ben shook his head. 'There's no one. A trick of the light, that's all. I shouldn't have told you all that nonsense about hauntings and such like. Peggy'll be furious with me. You take it from me, m'dear, that cottage is as empty as an underground cavern.'

Had it just been a trick of the light? Emma tried to believe it, but felt certain in her mind that the shadow crossing the window had been that of a person. The thought sent a chill of fear sweeping through her.

Chapter 3

Certain now that the present had just been a practical joke, and determined to deny Becky the pleasure of laughing at her, Emma decided to say nothing about her discovery of the empty cottage. She might have got away with it, had Mark not shown a sudden and strange interest in her that evening.

They had just finished the Black Forest gateau, which Aunt Peggy had bought for her birthday cake, and were relaxing in the small sitting room, when Mark glanced up from his motorbike magazine and murmured:

'Penny for them, Em.'

Emma started in surprise. 'What?'

'Penny for your thoughts,' said Mark again. 'You've been lost in them all evening.'

'Oh, have I?' Flustered, Emma patted the satin cushion and settled herself more comfortably in the armchair, in an attempt to play for time. 'Sorry.'

Aunt Peggy looked up from her writing desk anxiously. 'You're not worrying about things, are you dear? The doctors are certain your mother will be well again very soon.'

'Yes, I know. I wasn't worrying.'

But her aunt was still anxious and, in a vain effort to take Emma's mind off her worries, managed to put both feet right in it. 'Did you find that house, dear?'

Emma glanced quickly to where Becky sat. 'Yes. I saw Ben. He said he'd be in on Friday as usual.'

Her cousin was watching a film on the television and showed no interest in the conversation.

'Ben?' Aunt Peggy put down her pen and stared at her niece in surprise. 'When did you see him?'

'This afternoon. He was in his garden.'

'Oh?'

To stop her aunt from questioning further, Emma blurted, 'He was telling me about that girl. You know, the one who disappeared.'

She fancied she saw a faint flicker in Becky's cold eyes.

'Oh.' Aunt Peggy seemed surprised. 'Now what ever made him do that, I wonder?'

'It just came up in conversation.'

'How strange,' Aunt Peggy murmured. 'Goodness, I'd almost forgotten it myself.'

At her mother's words, Becky came to life with a vengeance. 'How could you forget? How *could* you, when it nearly ruined you.'

'Oh, do stop it, dear.' Aunt Peggy sounded weary, and slowly rubbed her eyes. 'Don't start raking that up all over again.'

'The gipsies took her, and they've been allowed to get away with it all these years.' Becky's voice was high-pitched.

Her mother looked angry. 'How can you say such terrible things? You know nothing, absolutely nothing. Why, you weren't even born.'

Becky looked at her sulkily. 'I know what people say.'

'You'd listen to anything rather than use your

own head.' Aunt Peggy folded her arms and sighed. 'You're just like all the others, prejudiced, superstitious and too quick to judge. Well, I've told you this once, and I'm telling you again. In this country, a person is innocent until proved guilty, and not the other way around. So please remember it in future.'

'Then how is it that everyone wants the gipsy camp moved?' Becky had no intention of letting the subject drop.

'I don't know why.' Aunt Peggy softened her speech in an effort to reason with the unreasonable. 'I daresay that some have good reasons to want to see them leave Swallow Field, but they've never done anyone any harm, not that we know about. And whether I approve of them or disapprove is not the point. I draw the line at dirty tricks. Using that girl's disappearance as an excuse to get them out was wicked. Had the townfolk been successful, those gipsies would have been sent packing with a terrible slur on them. It's dreadful to be blamed for a crime you didn't commit.'

'You don't know that they didn't do it,' cried Becky.

'You don't know that they did.' Aunt Peggy's voice was harsher now. 'Someone had to stand up for them.'

'But did it have to be you?' Becky looked at her brother for support. 'Look what it did to you and Dad.'

'That's right, Mum,' said Mark slowly. 'You lost most of your business to Perrings after that.'

Aunt Peggy shrugged. 'That was more than twenty

years ago. We got most of it back again, when tempers had cooled.'

Mark shook his head. 'I can remember Dad saying that you never got more than a quarter back.'

'That's what I've been saying . . .'

'Leave it, Becky,' snapped Mark. 'You've said quite enough for one evening.'

Mark's voice had suddenly assumed an authority which Emma would not have believed he possessed. Impressed, she stared at him, wondering if he was already, at fifteen, taking on the role of 'man of the house'. But he was a quiet soul; content to play cricket and dream of the day when he would own his first motorbike, rather than take an interest in the family business or keep his explosive sister under control.

'Who was it then, dear? Who sent the book?'

Emma saw her aunt staring at her and, unprepared for the sudden question, stammered, 'No one. Ninety-nine is empty.'

Too late. She could have bitten off her tongue. Becky, however, had turned her attention back to the television once more and showed no interest. How dare she? Emma felt anger rising within her. How dare she sit there calmly, after having stirred up this terrible row, and on her birthday, too!

'Empty?' Aunt Peggy was looking very surprised. 'Are you sure you went to the right house?'

Emma nodded. 'That's how I met Ben. It's the cottage right opposite to his.'

Mark looked up from his magazine once more. 'The old haunted place, do you mean?'

Emma shrugged and tried to sound casual. 'He did

32

mention something about it being haunted. But I don't believe in ghosts, so I just laughed.'

Aunt Peggy sounded confused. 'I don't understand. The book was from the lady at number ninety-nine.'

Emma smiled. 'The book was from Becky.'

On hearing her name, Becky looked round at them all. 'What was that?'

'Becky? Did you send Emma that book this morning?' Aunt Peggy sounded angry once more.

'No, of course not. Whatever makes you think I did?'

'Did you then, Mark?'

Mark put up his hands in mock resignation. 'Sorry. Practical jokes just aren't in my line, I'm afraid.' He stared at his sister. 'They never used to be in yours, either.'

'They're not now.' Becky looked thoroughly bewildered. 'I never sent you that book, Emma. What makes you think I did?'

She seemed so indignant, and so genuinely surprised, that Emma began to have doubts. 'Well then, there just has to be another ninety-nine, somewhere.'

'Not in Athelbury,' said Mark.

'Clearly the sender doesn't live here at all,' said Aunt Peggy.

Becky thought otherwise. 'She must do. How else would she have known about Emma's birthday in the first place? And don't forget she put the parcel on the counter as soon as you had opened the door almost. She must be local.'

Emma felt cold once more at the memory of the

unseen customer leaving the shop the previous morning. She tried to concentrate on the television, but kept hearing the clang of the bell as the thought churned around in her head. Soon, however, that thought blurred into another and the screen became a window with a shadowy figure moving across it.

She slept badly that night, but became less tense as the morning slipped by in a rush of hard work. Wednesday was delivery day in Athelbury and most of it was spent in the small stock room checking off newly-arrived boxes and unpacking. Much against her will Becky had been roped in to help, but her sullen manner caused a bad atmosphere and Emma, glad of the work, was not glad of her cousin's company.

The bombshell dropped as lunch ended. Aunt Peggy rose to clear away the plates and smiled down at the girls.

'How would you like a country walk this afternoon?'

Emma smiled with pleasure. The weather was still fine, though not so hot, and she was tired of being indoors. 'I'd love it.'

'Good. I need some more herbs from a friend of ours, and Becky knows where to go for them.' Aunt Peggy turned her attention to her daughter. 'Now I've already phoned Mary Ann, so she should have them all ready. I want sage, parsley, lavender and thyme.'

At the name of Mary Ann the smile vanished from Emma's face. The last thing on earth she wanted right now was contact with some cranky, superstitious woman who took delight in spreading doom and gloom. But the matter was clearly settled, and there seemed no good reason to refuse to go on this errand which would not risk upsetting both aunt and cousin.

So it was that Emma found herself heading out of Athelbury, down the cobble-stoned hill, past the terraced cottages on its steep slopes and into the wooded lane that led to the village of Cranmore, just two miles from the town. Tall beech trees on each side of the lane reached outwards to form a high arch overhead. She gazed up at the sun glittering through swaying branches and it seemed to her that she was walking along the nave of a cathedral.

Sheba was pulling excitedly on the leash, eager to chase off into the woods, but Becky held her firmly, ever-watchful for approaching cars. Only one passed by them, leaving the lane lonely and deserted once more.

'Is Mary Ann very old?'

But Emma's question remained unanswered. Startled by the sudden appearance of a youth from the trees, she jumped back. Becky held tightly on to Sheba, who started barking at the boy.

He was stocky and muscular, but not very tall; his hair was almost black and his eyes shone in a swarthy complexion. His red-checked shirt sleeves were rolled up to the elbow, and the brown corduroy trousers seemed large and were held at the waist by a leather belt. In one hand the gipsy boy carried a dead rabbit, while in the other he clasped an empty sack.

Becky swerved away and quickened her pace almost to a run, crying, 'Come on, Emma, come on!'

Staring at the gipsy nervously, Emma did the only thing she could do in the circumstances, and that was to catch up with her cousin as quickly as possible.

'It be only a dead rabbit!' the boy cried out after them.

'Becky,' Emma gasped. 'Why did you run off like that? You frightened me more than he did.'

'It's a lonely lane,' Becky murmured breathlessly. 'I won't come along it again on my own. Not with the likes of them hanging around.'

Emma was thirsty by the time they reached Cranmore, a village consisting of some twelve stone cottages grouped around a pond. Ducks of all breeds and sizes sat preening themselves on the grass banks, ignoring the horseman riding past on his dapple grey mare. He bade the girls a good afternoon then turned into Church Lane, leaving the air still and silent once more.

As they approached the pond some of the ducks started waddling towards them in the hope of bread. Their loud cries set off others until the whole village resounded to the noise which only died away as the girls turned into the twitchel that led between two cottages to a field. On the far side of a herd of Friesians stood a thatched cottage, surrounded by a rickety white fence. Tied to this fence was a brown goat who bleated her welcome at the girls approach.

'That's Mandy,' Becky said. 'We won't get too close to her, or Sheba will get jealous. Besides, she eats everything and anything.'

Becky tied the dog to the gate post and poked her head through the open doorway of the cottage.

'Hello, Mary Ann,' she called. There was no reply. 'She must be in the outhouse. That's where she dries her herbs. Come on, we'll wait inside.'

Emma hesitated. 'Won't she mind?'

Becky looked irritated by the remark. 'Of course not. Come on.'

Following her cousin into the small and untidy room, Emma felt, immediately, the overpowering heat from a black cooking range. Wondering why Mary Ann needed to light a fire on such a hot day, she screwed up her nose in distaste. 'What's that smell?'

Becky shrugged. 'Dandelion roots. She's drying them out in the oven. Then she'll crush them to make coffee powder.'

'Coffee? From dandelions?'

Mary Ann made no sound on entering. Only her figure blocking the light from the doorway made Emma swivel around in sudden fear, then stare in surprise. This was not the woman Becky's words had painted in her mind. That woman was old, wore long, dark clothes and had a thin, pointed nose. Standing before her, however, was a tall and fairly slim woman who wore her blonde hair tied back at the neck to hang straight down between her shoulders. Over black trousers she wore a blue shirt, and her face might almost have been handsome, had it not been for her eyes. There was something strange about those eyes, although Emma could not, at first, put a finger on what it was, exactly. Only when Mary Ann drew closer did she realize why they disturbed her so much. They were almost without colour, and put her in mind of a sheep.

Mary Ann said the usual, normal things, in a lilting

Dorset accent, but there was about her an air of remoteness that was not normal. If she connected Emma with the stranger who would bring fear and danger, then she did not betray her thoughts, but neither did she show friendliness or warmth.

As Becky spoke of her mother's needs, Emma looked about her curiously. A large ginger cat lay sleeping on the window sill, and before it the table was still cluttered with the remains of lunch. Books were everywhere, some on shelves, but mostly on tables and chairs. Emma inched her way towards the settee and gazed down at the volumes strewn haphazardly across it, in an effort to make out their titles. *Herbal Medicines, The Occult, Herbs and the Sorcerer,* and *Witchcraft in Dorset* seemed to make up Mary Ann's reading matter. Small wonder, thought Emma, that the woman was so strange.

'I'll get the herbs in a minute,' murmured Mary Ann, searching through a pile of papers in a desk drawer. At last she found the notebook she sought. 'They're in the outhouse, all ready for you.' She opened the book and sat down at the table to write down Mrs Travis's latest purchases. 'Take a pew. I won't be long.'

Such words seemed normal enough, and lulled Emma into a feeling of security. She sat down in the armchair beside the range, and regretted it instantly as her legs began to scorch from the heat of the fire. Twisting away, she suddenly caught Mary Ann's colourless eyes boring into her, and felt her heart turn over. She's reading my thoughts. I mustn't think, mustn't think. Find something to say. What? Anything.

'Is dandelion coffee like ordinary coffee?' Her voice was much too high.

'It's very good for you,' answered Becky, even though the remark had not been addressed to her. 'Mary Ann never drinks anything other than herbal infusions. Mary Ann says most of the food we eat is sheer poison.'

Emma wondered why Mary Ann did not answer for herself, instead of allowing Becky to dance attendance on her like some lady in waiting. Then it occurred to her that Becky was not so much a lady in waiting but more a witch's familiar. Shocked at the wicked thought, Emma nevertheless smiled to herself, for surely her cousin's feline characteristics fitted the role even more than those of the ginger tom. After all, if Becky had been born a cat, she would have been black, lithe and watchful. So was it strange, then, that she should choose this weird woman to befriend?

Emma started, aware suddenly that Mary Ann's eyes were upon her again. She must not think, she must not think. But it was too late.

Almost as though she had read each thought, Mary Ann said quietly:

'I must have someone to pass the knowledge on to. Herbs are the elixir of life. Some have strange mystic powers, known only to those born with the gift, while some are deadly poisonous. Many years ago, people were curing their ills with herbs, long before we had doctors. There is much to learn, and Becky learns well. She has the true gift.'

Emma was determined to remain unimpressed. No wide-eyed innocent she, as Mary Ann would soon discover. She wondered what her aunt would make of Becky's tutelage at the knee of this self-styled witch.

'My mother drinks chamomile tea. She swears it's very good for her. I suppose you drink that too.' There, she had done it. She had let them both know that many ordinary people also believed in herbs. There was nothing strange about it.

'I do,' said Mary Ann, closing the book and placing it in the drawer. 'I only keep Indian for reading the leaves. My grandmother taught me.'

'Will you read the leaves for Emma?'

Emma threw her cousin an angry glance. How could she? Stupid girl.

Mary Ann said nothing for a while. Instead, she stood looking down at Emma as though trying to decide whether to grant this request or not. At length her mind was made up.

'Alright then. But only Emma, mind.'

As she disappeared into the kitchen to make the tea, Emma turned on her cousin in anger. 'What on earth made you say that? Are you completely mad, or what?'

Becky feigned surprise and let a sly smile play on her lips. 'You mean you *don't* want to have your fortune told?'

'You know perfectly well that I don't!'

'Ssh. She's coming back.'

Emma sighed and folded her arms. Perhaps she was over-reacting, she told herself. Why not look on the bright side for a change? She might even learn something good. She might learn when her mother was coming out of hospital. Then an awful thought struck her. She might learn that her mother was not coming out at all.

'No, no. I really don't want her to do this, Becky. Let's say we've changed our minds.'

'You can't. She'll be angry. Sssh.'

At that moment Mary Ann returned, carrying two brown mugs which she handed to the girls without ceremony. Emma looked down at hers with distaste. The tea had no milk or sugar in it and the mug smelt badly, as though it had not been properly washed for days.

'Mary Ann doesn't believe in milk or sugar,' said Becky, looking at her cousin with obvious amusement. 'Mary Ann thinks both are causes of ill health.'

Oh, how she's enjoying this, thought Emma, sipping the bitter-tasting brew and wishing Becky would shut up. At last, she gladly handed the cup back to her hostess who then sat down in the armchair opposite and stared into the dregs. For a long time she said nothing, then she looked at Emma with something akin to alarm in those colourless eyes.

'Why did you come to this place?'

'My mother was taken ill. What is it? Is it something about my mother?' Emma became frightened. 'Is it something bad? Is she going to die?'

'Calm yourself, girl. Your mother's fate is not shown in the leaves. Is there no one at your own home?'

'My father, yes. But he's at work all day and . . . why? What is it?'

Mary Ann leaned forward and stared at Emma

earnestly. 'Go home, girl. Return to your own home, this very day.'

'Why?' gasped Emma.

'Because this is a bad town for you.'

'Athelbury?' Emma felt cold suddenly. 'Why do you say that?'

Mary Ann put down the cup and stood up. 'I've said too much already, and I make a point of not reading out misfortune.'

Becky sat forward on the edge of the settee. 'But Mary Ann! It's worse if you don't finish telling us. Just why is Athelbury a bad place for Emma?'

Mary Ann turned and stared out of the window. 'I do not mean to frighten you, girl. But heed my warning. Leave Athelbury, otherwise dreadful harm will befall you.'

Emma felt the blood draining from her face and glanced uneasily at Becky. Was she satisfied now, this cousin of hers who had clearly wanted to hear some such sensational revelation.

'What's going to happen to me, Mary Ann? If you tell, then I might be able to prevent it.'

Mary Ann shook her blonde head. 'It is written. There's no changing it. Not unless you leave. Maybe then, just maybe then . . .' Her voice trailed off. She turned and stared at Emma. 'There might be a way. You may laugh. You would, however, be foolish to discard my advice.'

Emma frowned. 'What? What is it? What can I do?'

'Come with me into the garden.'

Bewildered, the girls followed her out into the sunshine and along a narrow pathway dividing the sweetly-scented herbs. Bees hummed about them as they made their way past the large lavender bush towards the bottom of the garden. A strong smell of rosemary pervaded the air here, the shrub being so large it all but concealed the old stone wall of the outhouse. Beside this was a wooden gate, which stood ajar. Mary Ann closed it and shook her head.

'I could have sworn it was shut.'

She walked on, pausing at last beside an angelica plant. 'Now here is a powerful charm against evil forces.' She bent to the plant, plucked off a leaf stem and offered it to Emma. 'Wear angelica, child. Wear it day in and day out.'

Emma took the leaf stem and felt panic rising. 'But who wants to harm me?' she cried in a shrill voice. 'And how can a piece of herb protect anyone? It's impossible! It's just silly old medieval superstition.'

Mary Ann looked angered by this. 'Medieval, yes; silly, no. Wear it all the time. I'll fetch a safety pin and you can pin it to your clothes.'

At that moment they heard Sheba barking and hastened back to the gate where she had been tied. The gipsy boy stood there, holding high the sack to protect it from the bitch who kept leaping up at it.

'Call off your dog, lady,' the boy shouted.

'Sheba, down.' Becky's command had an instantaneous effect and the bitch fell to the ground, grumbling and whining as her nose twitched up at the bag held a few inches from it.

The boy moved away from the animal and walked towards Mary Ann. 'Any work for me, lady? I've strong arms and can turn them to anything.'

The reaction to his request was swift and surprisingly hostile. Mary Ann quivered with fury.

'Get off my land. Go on, get off or I'll call the law.'

The boy flashed angry dark eyes, but stood his ground.

'I only ask for work, lady, good honest work. I reckon you need some tidy 'elp around this place. The fence needs fixing, and I'm good with fences.'

'The best help you can give me, is to leave and never return. And that goes for all your people.' Mary Ann stood with her hands on her hips in an attitude of aggression. 'What's in the sack, then? Been poaching, gipsy?'

'He has,' said Becky. 'He's got a dead rabbit in there.'

'I didn't poach. We 'ave the right. It's written down. We 'ave the right to any game in Swallow Field and Monkton Wood 'ard by. We don't take much. Just a rabbit now and then.'

'Don't take much!' Mary Ann's voice was filled with loathing. 'You only took my inheritance and robbed me of married life.'

'And the girl,' urged Becky. 'Don't forget the girl.'

Emma shot a black look at her cousin. 'Stop it, Becky. What's the matter with you?'

'Go on, leave, or I'll call the police at once.' Mary Ann advanced towards the boy menacingly.

'Goujos.' The boy spoke through clenched teeth and turned away. 'I done you no hurt. Goujos.' He slung the sack over his shoulder and walked back to the twitchel with head held high.

Emma watched him go with deep misgivings. She felt sorry for him, and embarrassed for Mary Ann's rudeness. What a bigot the woman was! No wonder Becky was so strange and impossible at times.

'What did he call us?' Mary Ann sounded very put about.

'Goujos,' Becky answered. 'That's their name for non-gipsies. They don't like us calling them gipsies, but they don't mind calling us names.'

'Don't they like being called gipsies?' asked Emma. 'Why not?'

Becky shrugged. 'Mum says they think it's an insult. They call themselves "travellers".'

Mary Ann said she was sick and tired of what *they* liked and did not like, and went to fetch the packets of herbs for the girls to take home.

'They're in the outhouse. Wait there.'

Emma watched her go. 'Did Mary Ann realize she was insulting him by using the word?'

'I expect so.'

'Then why did she do it? And why was she so horrid to the boy? I mean, she can't blame him for something that you say happened a long time ago. He's only about Mark's age, for goodness sake!' She twirled the angelica around in her fingers once more. 'Fancy giving me this to ward off evil! What an idiot I'd look walking around town with this pinned to my clothes. The woman's a superstitious bigot, and I don't think she's good for you, Becky. You should stop seeing her.'

Becky put a hand on the restless fingers. 'Don't throw the angelica away. You'd really be tempting providence then. Believe me, if she says there's something rotten in the air, then there's something rotten. You'll find out . . .'

'They've gone! They've gone.' Mary Ann came racing from the outhouse, shouting at the top of her voice. 'He's stolen them, that gipsy thief has stolen my herbs!' She approached them breathlessly. 'I knew I had closed that gate. But I didn't close the outhouse door when you came. That boy had already been in there. I knew he had more than a rabbit in that sack. Just let him wriggle out of this one. I'll get on to the police at once.'

Chapter 4

'What did she mean by it?' Emma was staring into Cranmore pond, but saw nothing in its dark, murky depths. 'What did Mary Ann mean by the gipsies stealing her inheritance and robbing her of married life?'

Becky picked her way carefully among four Aylesbury ducks, which were waddling about her feet, to stand beside her cousin.

'That's just what they did too. Apparently her father once led a deputation calling for the gipsies to be thrown out of Swallow Field, so one old man, the leader of the gipsies hereabouts, put a curse on him. He said that, within six months, Mary Ann's father would be a ruined, sick man, and that his line would die out with his one and only child, a daughter. Well, within six months all their cattle had died from foot and mouth, and although the Government gave them compensation Mary Ann's father was too ill to start again. Mary Ann has never married, so there'll be no children to carry on the line. The curse has come true.'

Emma nodded. 'Which explains her hatred of gipsies.' She watched a small girl, on the far side of the pond, tossing pieces of bread to the ducks. 'But there must have been other farmers who lost their herds from foot and mouth. Still, I daresay Mary Ann forgot to tell you that. What's more, I can't imagine any man wanting to marry a woman like her, anyway. She'd give him the creeps.'

Becky looked angry. 'The reason she never married was because she sacrificed her youth to look after her sick father.'

Emma felt the shame she was meant to feel. 'Well, then, I'm sorry.' She turned to her cousin and shook her head. 'Nevertheless, you shouldn't believe all she tells you.'

The ducks, surrounding them now, suddenly made a dash for the pond. The girls watched as they swam towards the child on the other side, attacking each other in their efforts to reach the bread she was throwing.

'You refuse to believe anything,' said Becky, coldly. 'I knew you were coming here, but you refuse to believe that. Mary Ann warns of danger. I tell you of the gipsies' curse. You refuse to believe anything.'

Emma was quiet during the rest of their walk home. The incident with the gipsy boy had, momentarily at least, chased away the fear that Mary Ann's words had caused. Now, however, there was time to think, and that was the last thing she really wanted, for no matter which way her thoughts turned they always came back to the book and the empty cottage.

Two customers were in the shop when the girls returned, and Aunt Peggy left the one she was serving to tell Becky to put the herbs straight into the basket where they were always displayed. But Becky paused dramatically, shook her head and delighted in the sudden attention turned upon her. 'There are no herbs. They've been stolen by the gipsies.'

Shocked silence greeted this news, broken at length by an angry woman.

'Gipsies again! They're a disgrace to this town. It's high time the council did something.'

'But fancy stealing herbs,' said a younger woman. 'I mean to say – herbs!'

'Just the thing they *would* steal,' the other added. 'They can sell them, along with the heather. What are you going to do about it, Mrs Travis?'

But Aunt Peggy had barely recovered from her surprise. 'What happened, Becky?'

Conscious of the eyes on her, Becky explained in a loud voice, exaggerating here and there for a more dramatic effect. This angered Emma, but she was loathe to cause embarrassment to her relations by pointing out the errors in her cousin's account to the appalled listeners.

'Anyway,' said Becky, reaching the end of her strange story at last, 'Mary Ann's calling the police and they'll have to do something now.'

'Meanwhile,' sighed Aunt Peggy, 'we've no more herbs.'

She finished serving her customers, and gestured to Becky to go up to the flat. Emma guessed she did not want her daughter saying anything more about the incident in front of strangers.

Becky took the hint, grudgingly, and turned at the doorway. 'I'll make some tea. Come up in five minutes, and I'll hold the fort.'

Emma stood in the kitchen watching her cousin pour boiling water into the teapot. 'Why did you do it? Why did you exaggerate so?'

'Exaggerate?' Becky put the lid on the teapot and

covered it with the knitted cosy her mother had made some ten years earlier. 'I never exaggerate.'

'You did. You told those people that the boy chased us. He didn't. We ran, but he didn't chase us.'

Becky took a bottle of milk from the refrigerator, poured some into a small jug and placed it on the tray with the sugar bowl, cups and saucers.

'He was going to. I could sense it.'

It was useless, thought Emma, picking up the tray and carrying it into the sitting room. Becky was prepared to spin a yarn simply because there were many ears ready to believe anything she said. The truth would be too dull for them; and they would only shake their heads, anyway, saying, 'There's no smoke without fire.'

Aunt Peggy was coming up the stairs as Becky was about to start down them. She stood back for her mother to pass, then turned as a disapproving voice said, 'We'll talk about this business later on, dear, but please don't say another word about it to anyone.'

At that moment the shop bell clanged loudly. Becky shrugged. 'Ah well, at least I shan't have time to get bored.'

She walked on down, but at the threshold stopped dead in her tracks.

Aunt Peggy looked over the landing and frowned. 'Well go on, child. Don't keep the customers waiting.'

'There's no one there.' Becky's voice was thin and shaky.

'But I heard the bell.'

'There's a book on the counter, and it's tied with red ribbon.'

Her mother came down the stairs at once, followed by Emma who had overheard the brief conversation. All three walked into the deserted shop and stared at the package on the counter, as though touching it might cause an electric shock. At length Aunt Peggy picked it up, untied the ribbon and opened the book. She was silent for a while, then closed the book and handed it to Emma.

'It seems, my dear, that you have another present.'

Emma's heart missed a beat. Dismay written all over her face, she took the book from her aunt and gazed at the picture of a small girl weeping beside a stream. It was faded, and the dark red of the cover had become discoloured with age.

'*The Courage of Faith*,' murmured Aunt Peggy, peering over Emma's shoulder. 'Well, she certainly does pick them, whoever she is.'

Emma opened the book, saw the familiar shaky scrawl on the fly-leaf and read aloud: 'To Emma. With kindest thoughts, from the lady at 99.'

There was a long silence, followed by Emma's shaky laugh.

'It's a joke. Someone's kidding me . . . someone's having a laugh at my expense.' She tried to force a smile, but found she had no control over her trembling lips. 'Is it Mary Ann?'

Becky took the book, read the inscription, then put it back on the counter, shuddering visibly. 'She warned us. She said fear and danger. Well, this certainly frightens me.' Ashen faced, she edged away

51

from her cousin, then rushed through the doorway and up the stairs.

'What did Becky mean?' asked Aunt Peggy, looking anxious. 'What did she mean, Mary Ann warned you? Warned you about what?'

The conversation stopped abruptly as a small boy entered the shop. He walked over to the counter, stood on tip-toe and put several coins down on the top. No more than six years of age, the child's T-shirt rode up as he stretched, leaving a band of exposed waist between it and his blue cotton trousers.

Aunt Peggy leaned over the counter and smiled at the golden head below her.

'Hello, Tommy. Shopping for Mummy again? What does she want? Have you a note?'

'Butter. She wants half a pound of butter, please.'

Emma stood smiling down also at the little boy. 'Hello, Tommy. My name's Emma. Did you see anyone coming out of the shop just now?'

The child stared up at her with solemn grey eyes and shook his head slowly from side to side.

'No one at all?' asked Emma.

'No.'

'He lives by Ben's cottage. You were there yesterday,' said Aunt Peggy, putting the butter into a white paper bag.

'That far? Isn't he a little young to be out in all this traffic?'

'His mother works in the launderette, next door. Tommy stays with her, when he isn't in school. He often pops in to get some shopping. There we are, my lad. Careful how you go now.'

As Tommy left, Emma sighed and folded her

arms. 'Pity. I had hoped he might have seen someone. I must have been mad not to look myself. It just didn't occur to me, until it was too late.'

At that moment Mark walked in from the street. Once again, his jeans were covered in grease stains and, at his mother's cry of consternation, he raised his hands in the air.

'No sweat, no sweat. It's only grease from Graham's scooter.'

'Only! Do you know how much trouble I have getting it off?' Aunt Peggy shook her head. 'Well, this time it's your problem. You'll find eucalyptus oil in the bathroom cupboard, but mind you do it outside in the garden or you'll stink the place out.'

'Right. No hassle. I'll do it. But what's all this I hear about gipsies raiding Mary Ann's cottage? Did they get away with much?'

'Herbs.' Becky's voice, from the back of the room, made Emma turn in surprise, since she had not heard her return. At once, and ignoring her mother's wish to say no more about it in the shop, Becky continued with her dramatic story in a voice so loud that customers, coming in at that point, became so interested they almost forgot why they had entered in the first place.

'Now just how did *you* know?' asked Emma, gazing up at Mark in puzzlement.

'It's all over town.' Mark looked thoughtful as he stared out of the large window. 'Did you say this lad was carrying a sack?'

'Yes. Why?' answered Becky.

'Red shirt?'

'I think so.'

'Must be him. He was in the street just now.' Mark's eyes were scanning the shoppers passing by. Suddenly, they opened wide. 'There he is now. Coming out of Perrings as cheeky as you like. He's walking across the road. Looks like he's coming this way.' With that, Mark rushed out of the shop.

Emma exchanged worried glances with her aunt, but Becky peered through the window crying, 'He's gone up to the boy! Mark's got him in a half-nelson.' The voice rose to a pitch of excitement. 'He's bringing him in here.'

The shop bell clanged; the door burst open and into the shop, arm held firmly behind him by Mark, marched the gipsy boy. He stared at the group in bewildered alarm.

'Well. Is this the boy?' asked Mark.

'Yes!' cried Becky. 'That's him, that's the thief.'

'Let him be.' Aunt Peggy came from behind the counter. 'You're hurting the boy, Mark. Let him be.' As Mark released the frightened youth, she stood staring at him with eyes that were gentle yet firm. 'Now then. What is your name?'

'Eddy,' came the bold reply. 'And I'm no thief.' The dark eyes darted from face to face, then to the doorway, only to find escape barred by Mark's tall frame.

'Look in the sack,' said Becky. 'Go on, look in the sack.'

The boy swung around to face her, then set his lips in an expression of contempt. 'You again,' he hissed. 'Why, you're nothing but a lying, stupid . . .'

'Don't you speak to my sister that way,' said Mark, moving in on the boy.

54

'That's right,' said a young woman customer. 'You tell him.'

'Why not make him turn out the sack, then?' asked an elderly man.

Eddy stood silent for a while, then slowly turned to Becky, grinned, held the sack high and tipped the dead rabbit out on to her feet, laughing as she screamed.

'Get it off, get it off!'

'That's all I 'ave in the sack.' Eddy turned it inside out. 'What is it I'm supposed to 'ave stolen?'

'He's got rid of them already,' snorted Becky. 'I'll bet he's sold them. I'll bet he's sold them to Perrings.'

'I went in there to buy tea and sugar,' said Eddy grimly. 'I paid good money for them an' all.' He held up a brown paper bag which clearly contained his purchases. 'I got a receipt in here.'

'I daresay you have,' snapped Becky. 'But where did the money come from?'

'Shhh, Becky.' Aunt Peggy looked confused and unsure what to do next. 'Look after him, Mark. I must phone Mary Ann.' She turned to the customers. 'Would you mind bearing with me for a moment? We really can't go on like this.'

Everyone watched in silence as she walked into the passageway and picked up the telephone. Then the customers turned to each other, murmuring.

'It's time matters were brought to a head.'

'Start a petition going, that's what I say. Make the council do something.'

'I hear they're going to make Swallow Field a permanent site for gipsies.'

55

'What? That's disgraceful! We pay our rates. Why should we put up with it?'

Emma only half-listened to their disgruntled mutters; the rest of her concentration was centred on the voice coming from the passageway.

'You've found what?' Aunt Peggy sounded amazed and was shouting rather loudly. 'But how did that happen? And the fence is broken? How many packets did she eat? Good gracious. Will she be alright?' A long pause followed and then Aunt Peggy dropped her voice so low that Emma found it difficult to hear. 'Well . . . yes, but it's most unfortunate because . . . here. Yes . . . now . . . accused him . . .'

The deathly silence in the shop did not help Aunt Peggy as she returned to face the boy. She looked angry and highly embarrassed as she clasped and unclasped her hands.

'I'm sorry, Eddy. You *were* telling the truth, after all.'

'What is it?' shouted Becky. 'What did Mary Ann say?'

Her mother looked at her angrily and raised a hand to calm her noisy daughter. 'Just settle down. It seems that our thief turned out to be a nanny goat. Mandy, apparently, has broken away from the fence and caused havoc in the drying room. She's eaten several packets of herbs and scattered the others all over the place. Mary Ann says that when she first walked into the outhouse and saw that the bench, where she had placed the herbs, was empty, she didn't even think about the goat, and rather jumped to conclusions.'

Eddy listened to her apologies, then bent to pick up the dead rabbit. As he put it back in the sack, he stared darkly at everyone.

'Tis no more than we've come to expect. You steal, too, but you don't pull one of your kind off the streets yelling "thief". No, you'd find proof before you accused a Goujo.' He turned wild, flashing eyes on Becky and Emma. 'Don't 'ee stand in my way no more.' With that, he flung the sack over his shoulder and left the shop.

There was a long and awkward silence, broken at last by one of the more timid women. 'Even so, I still say you can't trust them an inch.'

'I've never been so embarrassed in all my life.' Mark came storming into the sitting room after his indignant sister. 'Why didn't you check out every possibility before telling the world you'd found a thief?'

'How was I to know?' Becky threw herself on to the settee and folded her arms dramatically. 'After all, I wasn't the one to drag the boy in off the street. You could find yourself up for assault, Mark Travis.'

Emma picked up the teapot from the side table, realized it was now cold and took it into the kitchen to make a fresh brew.

If only they hadn't gone to Mary Ann's, she thought, then this awful thing wouldn't have happened. They had been unkind, cruel even, to a boy they knew nothing about, simply because he was a gipsy. That made him different, and people who were different were seemingly not welcome in this or any other community.

Becky and Mark were still arguing when she

returned to the sitting room with the fresh tea. She felt bound to speak her mind at last.

'Your mother told me they were true Romany gipsies, proud people who kept their homes spotless and lived independent lives. They're not layabouts, thieves and scallawags.'

Becky looked up at her as though she had been stung. 'Go on, rub it in. Anyway you're talking through the back of your head. A gipsy, is a gipsy, is a gipsy. They're all as bad as each other. Don't forget how that girl vanished, and don't forget what happened to Mary Ann's father. Now I expect they'll put a curse on *us*.'

'Oh, leave off, Becky,' said Mark pouring out the tea. 'You talk like some housewife from the Middle Ages.'

'No, it's true!' Becky was on her feet now, as though her own words had come into focus and she could see very clearly some terrible vengeance being hurled at them from afar. 'They have the power, and they won't forgive us. They'll do something, something bad. You'll see.'

Aunt Peggy came into the room and Mark went down to guard the shop. She said nothing to her daughter, but sat down in an armchair and gratefully accepted the cup of tea Emma handed to her. Then she peered at her niece and frowned.

'What's that in your blouse?'

Emma looked down in surprise and saw the herb pinned to her pocket. She blushed with embarrassment. 'It's angelica.'

'Angelica?' Aunt Peggy looked astonished. 'Why on earth are you wearing it, dear? It's all limp now.'

'Mary Ann insisted, and I didn't like to offend her.'

Too tired, and too confused, to pursue this strange answer, Aunt Peggy shook her head and sipped her tea. 'Well, dear, it looks very odd.'

Emma unpinned it from her blouse and placed it on the coffee table, glad that her aunt was too weary to question her further. Peace descended on the room while they both drank their tea in silence. Becky remained curled up on the settee, her arms folded tightly, her lips set hard against the world.

'What did you mean by Mary Ann *warning* you?' Aunt Peggy's sudden question came like a thunder bolt, and Emma nearly dropped her cup. 'Warning you about what?'

'Oh, just something she saw in the leaves.' Emma tried to sound casual and unconcerned. 'I think it's all a lot of nonsense.'

'I hope she hasn't been upsetting you, dear. She's a bit eccentric, although she means well, I suppose. She believes the strangest things. Old folklore and the like. She once told Mark that Stonehenge was built by the Devil. He brought the stones from Ireland to arrange in a circle, as a kind of joke. But apparently he was spotted by a priest who taunted him. This made Satan very angry, so he started hurling the stones about, and one caught the priest on the heel as he was running away. That's why it's called the Heel Stone, today.' She laughed. 'Poor Mark. He believed every word for years. Of course, he was only seven when she told him. So you see, my dear, we take Mary Ann with a pinch of salt.'

Becky glared at her mother, but said nothing.

Taking comfort from Aunt Peggy's words,

Emma's thoughts again turned to the book. 'I left it downstairs. If only we could find out who sent it.'

'You know who sent it.' Becky's voice was strained and barely audible.

Her mother turned and stared at her disapprovingly. 'No more, Becky. I think we've all heard quite enough from you for one day. I'll talk to you later.'

'I might have got it wrong about the boy,' said Becky, 'but I know I'm right over this. I feel it. There's something very weird going on, and it frightens me.'

Emma bit her bottom lip nervously. 'Just *what* do you think is going on?'

'It isn't a joke on our part, and no one else, apart from Mary Ann, knows you. Yet you have received two books from a dead woman and a seer predicts that something bad is going to happen to you if you stay here.'

'What?' Aunt Peggy jumped to her feet. 'Did Mary Ann say that to Emma?'

Becky shrugged. 'She was only trying to help her.'

'But it's nonsense,' cried Emma, feeling fear rising within her once more. 'Even if there are such things as ghosts, they walk through walls – they don't send presents.'

'This wasn't sent,' said Becky quietly. 'This was delivered personally, and so was the other one.'

Aunt Peggy listened to her daughter in growing astonishment. 'I can hardly believe I'm hearing this conversation. Good heavens, girl, what are you thinking?'

'You've heard of poltergeists, haven't you?' Becky could not understand her mother's attitude. 'Well

60

then, if spirits like those can throw furniture around, why not a book?'

'What, and then write in it, tie a red ribbon round it, and bring it to this shop?' said Emma.

Aunt Peggy smiled. 'Don't you think that someone might have noticed a parcel wafting along the High Street on it's own?'

'Not if the person bringing it could be seen too,' said Becky. 'And who would look twice at an old lady?'

Emma's eyes opened wide with horror. 'You're joking. You don't really believe what you're saying, surely?'

'Yes I do.'

Unable to think of an answer, Emma could only snap 'Rubbish!' as she dashed out of the room.

It was hot and sultry in the back garden, but Emma had to get out of the house, away from her anxious aunt, her dark-minded cousin and that wretched book. All she wanted now was to be alone, to have time to think and try to settle her mind.

Sinking into a faded deck chair, she felt comforted that Mark had also come into the garden and was now cleaning his bike beside the garden shed; but not comforted enough to rid her mind of its growing fears. She felt singled out. Someone, a woman she did not know, knew her and seemingly wanted to frighten her. Why? All this, in itself, was unnerving, but added to Mary Ann's dire predictions it became positively frightening.

A shimmering heat haze lay over the vale, and the only sound breaking the stillness of the hour was a lark singing high above. Slowly Emma began to relax. The hot sun made her sleepy and the sultriness made breathing difficult. Her head began to droop, her eyelids became heavy, and she watched Mark through half-closed eyes.

Suddenly a shadow passed before her. Emma looked up and saw the dark silhouette of someone standing against the bright sun. Putting a hand to her brow, she tried to see who it was, but the silhouette vanished at once, leaving her staring into the glaring rays once more. She sat up quickly and gazed about her. There was no one in the garden save for Mark and herself.

'Where is she?' Emma cried, jumping to her feet.

'Who?'

'The woman. I saw a woman . . . at least I think it was.'

Mark was kneeling beside the bicycle. 'You must have been dreaming. There wasn't anyone.'

Panic rose in Emma's throat. 'But there was, I saw her.'

'It's the heat.' Mark wiped his greasy hands on an old rag. 'It can cause optical illusions, like a mirage. That's what you saw.'

A mirage? Emma felt very shaken and sat down again, trying to hold on to the thought. A mirage. Yes, of course. What else? Thank goodness for Mark. Calm, dependable Mark, as unlike his superstitious sister as the sun to the moon. She closed her eyes once more and felt the warm sun lulling her into a drifting half-sleep. Through the snatches of dreams came a picture of a drooping leaf stem lying on a coffee table, and one stabbing thought: 'This wasn't sent, it was delivered personally.'

Chapter 5

Unable to settle after the incident in the garden, Emma asked if she could take Sheba for a walk. Her aunt, however, seeing that Emma was not quite herself, insisted on Becky going with her.

She means well, thought Emma, pulling back on the leash in a vain effort to keep the excitable bitch under control. But if only I could be left alone. She sighed and accepted her lot, which was to walk side by side with a sullen girl who was still nursing a grievance.

'Alright, I'm sorry,' said Emma at last. 'I shouldn't have snapped your head off, I suppose, but what with one thing and another . . .'

'What makes you think it's any the more pleasant for me?' cut in Becky sharply. 'I was only trying to help, but since you think that everything I say is nonsense, I shan't bother to say another word. Everyone's against me today.'

They walked on in silence until they came to the Market Square. It was becoming more and more humid. Beads of perspiration stood on Emma's brow. She began to realize that Sheba was pulling them towards the lane and found herself doing nothing to make the animal change course. Some strange compulsion driving her on, she followed the animal past the cricket field on the right and down the hill until they saw the hazy, sundrenched vale spread out before them. She slowed her pace, wondering why she had come back here. What could she possibly hope to learn from it?

Becky glanced at her curiously, then broke her moody silence.

'Don't tell me, let me guess. We're going to the cottage so that you can prove to me just how you don't believe in ghosts.'

Is that what she was doing? Emma considered this as a motive, then rejected it. Trying to prove anything to Becky had been the last thing on her mind, but now it seemed she had been challenged to do just that.

They came to the cottage, paused by the ramshackle gate and looked in at the wilderness that had once been a well cared for garden. The tangle of nettles and long grass ended with a tall hedge of brambles which ran along the rear of the dwelling. Blackberries grew in abundance here, large healthy fruit that would soon ripen and yet seemed destined only for birds and field mice. In some places the hedge was broken, revealing a glimpse of the vale beyond, while the garden as a whole was dominated by a large chestnut tree, its branches shading most of the area to the right of the outbuildings.

Becky commanded Sheba to sit, then turned to Emma. 'Are you sure this *is* ninety-nine?'

Emma nodded. 'Ben said it was. A Mrs Bennett used to live here, apparently.'

'And her ghost haunts!' Becky murmured, looking back at the cottage.

Emma forced a laugh. 'If you believe in ghosts, you might believe that. But you know what I think.'

'I believe it. I've always believed it. I never thought to ask her name, though. Isn't that strange?' Becky shuddered, then let her eyes slide from the cottage to her cousin. 'Well?'

'Well what?'

'Aren't you going to prove to me that you're not afraid of her?' There was a whisper of a smile on Becky's lips. 'Or *are* you afraid, and just won't admit it.'

Emma stiffened. 'Of course I'm not. But how am I supposed to prove it, for goodness sake?' Since Becky made no answer to this, she went on. 'Oh well, if I have to go trespassing just to prove a point, then I'll just have to go trespassing. Here, you look after Sheba, unless you want to come in as well.'

Becky shook her head. 'No way.'

Being half off its hinges, the gate would not yield until both girls pushed together. Then, as Emma squeezed through the narrow opening, she heard Sheba growling and looked round quickly.

'What's the matter with her?'

Becky bent to the bitch and calmed her. 'I don't know. She doesn't usually carry on like this. Look, she's trembling.'

Emma looked at the frightened animal, then up at the window, half expecting to see another shadowy movement, but there was nothing. Yet everyone knew that dogs were highly sensitive to anything abnormal. Suddenly a large pigeon flew out of the chestnut tree, and Emma's shoulders sagged with relief.

'That's all it was. A pigeon.'

'Don't go in there.' Becky sounded frightened. 'I was only kidding. Don't go in, please.'

But, overcome with curiosity now, Emma was already halfway along the garden path and forcing her way through the overgrown weeds. Testing the latch on the shabby front door, she found it locked, and turned her attention to the window on the right. Peering through the dirty pane, she saw a room that was cold, empty and covered with dust and cobwebs. Opposite was a small brick fireplace with white wooden shelves set into alcoves on either side of it. Emma tried to imagine how it would have looked with a roaring fire, porcelain on the shelves, chintz-covered chairs and small polished tables. At length she turned away, not wishing to dwell on the sad, dead room it had now become.

Ignoring Becky's pleas to come away, Emma walked on towards the back of the building and came face to face with the crumbling outhouse. The door here was not locked, and yielded to her gentle push.

She stood staring into semi-darkness until her eyes could make out the pile of firewood standing in the far corner. A tin bath hung from a nail in the wall and beside it a long coil of rope which had once served as a clothes line. Next to this was a small bag made of sacking, still filled with pegs. Everything was neat and tidy, and only the cobwebs on the gardening tools told a casual visitor that Mrs Bennett was no longer bustling about her home, keeping it clean and ship-shape.

Emma closed the door and walked to the rear of the cottage. Standing on tip-toe she tried to peer through a small window but was suddenly aware of the frightening fact that someone was watching her.

Turning swiftly, she looked this way and that. The garden was empty. Nervous, watchful, and tense as a cornered rabbit, she stared at the bramble hedge for any sign of movement. There was no movement, no sound, yet the feeling was still there, strong and overwhelming. Someone was watching every move she made.

She must have taken a step or two backwards, for suddenly she felt the door give way behind her, and staggered into the cottage. Though shaken at first, Emma recovered quickly and turned around to find herself inside the kitchen. It smelt dank and musty. Cooking fumes from the ancient gas stove had discoloured the once green walls and the red tiles on the floor were worn and cracked.

Curious to see the rest of the cottage, yet alert and apprehensive, Emma stood still, listening intently. Whoever had opened this back door might still be here, she thought. On the other hand, Becky was not far away, so what harm could come to her anyway?

Curiosity finally getting the better of common sense, she crept out of the kitchen and into the dark and narrow hall. Two rooms led off at the bottom of the stairway. The first she had already viewed through the window, and the other proved as empty as the first. Emma turned her attention to the stairs.

Pausing with one hand on the brown bannister, she stood, uncertain. Was it safe? Weird thoughts crowded her mind, hidden fears drawn from deep within her. She fought them down and started climbing. A stair creaked beneath her weight, standing her hair on end, but soon she was on the landing and staring at three brown doors. One was closed, another ajar, while the third stood open wide enough to beckon.

Emma walked through it and found herself in the front bedroom, the very room where she had seen the shadow move across the window. It was empty enough now. The rose-patterned wallpaper was badly faded and over the black iron fireplace was a pale square where a picture had once hung. Emma's eyes were drawn down to the grate, and came to rest on a brown paper bag and several pieces of tissue paper. She was just about to investigate further, when she felt her blood turn to ice. Someone was humming.

Rooted to the spot with fear, she slowly turned her head towards the door. There was no mistaking it now, someone was in the other bedroom. The humming was low but the tune quite recognizable as a song Emma once sang in school called 'The Raggle Taggle Gipsies'.

Becky! The sudden thought sent a wave of relief through her. Of course. Becky was up to her old tricks and trying to frighten her again. Suddenly finding life in her limbs, Emma moved over to the window. Her cousin was still standing at the gate with Sheba.

Horrified, Emma spun round to face the bedroom door. Her legs felt weak, her hands became clammy and her heart raced. Ben's words rushed into her mind: 'He put tenants in once, but they were out within a week, saying they had seen things.'

What things? What would she see in that other

68

room? If only she had brought the angelica with her. If only she had listened to Becky and Mary Ann. If only . . . if only . . .

It was too late. She moved slowly towards the door. The humming seemed louder. Edging out on to the landing and keeping flat against the wall, Emma crept towards the second bedroom. The hummer was now singing, in a low, melancholy voice.

> 'Last night you slept in a goose feather bed,
> With the sheet turned down so bravely O.
>
> Tonight you'll sleep in an open field,
> Along with the Raggle Taggle Gipsies O.'

The singing stopped. Emma prayed silently, then steeled herself to push open the door and peer around the edge.

She was faced with an empty room. Moving in quickly, she gazed about her in astonishment, certain that the voice had come from here. At that moment, the humming started again. Emma swung around to face the door, realizing now that the voice came from the third room.

Her nerve failed her. Nothing on this earth would persuade her to enter that room. There was silence, then suddenly the stair creaked. Emma froze with terror. The stair creaked again. The hairs on her neck bristled.

Spurred into action, Emma crept swiftly out of the room and peered over the bannister. No one was on the stairs. Yet there *was* someone. There had to be.

Throwing all caution to the wind, she ran down

the staircase, hurled herself into the kitchen, just in time to see the back door closing. When she emerged into the sunlight she found the garden empty, and to her cries of, 'Did you see her, did you see her?' Becky merely replied with a puzzled look. Panting for breath, Emma drew close to the gate.

'But she must . . . she must have come this way. You must have seen her.'

'Nobody's come this way. Who am I supposed to have seen?'

Emma stood gasping. 'I . . . I don't understand. There's no other way out.'

Becky looked puzzled and frowned. 'But who? What happened? Tell me.'

At last Emma told her cousin all that had happened and saw the expression of puzzlement change to one of fear.

'But no one came out,' cried Becky. 'Which means that whoever it is must still be inside. And you say you saw no one?' She gave a quick tug on the leash. 'Let's go home.'

They wandered back along the lane, both lost in their thoughts but neither pressing the other to voice them. Before they turned the bend, however, Emma looked back once more to the dark, haunting windows of number ninety-nine. They seemed like eyes, watching and waiting. She shuddered and turned away.

Chapter 6

That night a storm rolled in from Somerset and circled about for hours before striking down upon the sleeping town. One by one, the bedroom lights came on and disturbed sleepers stared out at torrential rain gushing downhill to find no outlets in the over flowing drains. 'There'll be flooding down at Cranmore,' they murmured.

Lying with her head beneath the covers, Emma listened to the loud thunder, praying that the chimney would not come crashing down through the roof on to her bed.

But her fear of storms was nothing in comparison to the growing fear in her mind that something unnatural and sinister was happening to her in this Dorset town. Perhaps Mary Ann was right after all, and Athelbury would become the dangerous place she had predicted.

Emma jumped as another loud crack of thunder seemed to split the sky right over her head, then lay with her eyes shut, trying to reason with herself. There was no reason to feel this way. After all, no one had harmed her. Why should anyone wish to, anyway? Yet, for all her reasoning, Emma could not shake off the terrible foreboding which engulfed her once again. The thoughts, turning in her mind, kept homing in on the cottage and the unseen singer.

The voice had been young, in her opinion, which ruled out the absurd notion of ghosts. Whoever had been humming and singing had been real enough. Who, then? A squatter, perhaps? She remembered the rubbish in the grate and realized now that it must have been put there quite recently.

At breakfast, Aunt Peggy looked concerned as she spread marmalade on her toast.

'You don't look well, Emma. Aren't you going to eat anything?'

'No, thank you. I'll just have coffee, if you don't mind.'

Aunt Peggy poured coffee into her niece's cup and shook her head wearily. 'I'm not surprised. After that storm, we'll all be walking around like zombies today. You could have stayed in bed a little longer, dear. Becky and Mark have. Thursday's early closing anyway, and we don't usually have many customers in the morning.'

Emma smiled and gazed out of the window at the dull, dismal sky. 'I'd rather be busy.'

'I know,' said Aunt Peggy sympathetically. 'It helps to take your mind off things. Still, your father sounded much happier on the phone last night. Goodness, if your mother goes on improving at this rate, she'll be home sooner than you think.'

'How kind she is,' thought Emma, watching as her aunt left the room to open up the shop, 'and how happy I could have been here under different circumstances.' It seemed strange to her, now, that only five days ago she had entered Athelbury for the first time, knowing nothing then of number ninety-nine or Mary Ann. They had not entered her life.

But how quickly life can change. She would never take anything for granted again.

It happened just before lunch, as Aunt Peggy searched the back garden for a good-sized lettuce and Emma plucked large ripe tomatoes that grew in abundance by the south facing wall. Both heard the shop bell clang in the distance, but Mark had been left in charge during these last ten minutes before closing time so they could relax and chat to each other.

'I hate earwigs,' Aunt Peggy was saying. 'It's all these dahlias and asters. The earwigs love them so. I'm going to ask Mary Ann if there's a herb I can grow that will keep them away. I'm sure there must be.'

Emma stood up with the bowl of tomatoes and looked about her. The dullness of the morning was beginning to lift. It was much warmer and a misty haze now covered the vale, bringing with it the promise of very hot weather once more. She turned, saw Mark standing by the doorway, and nearly dropped the bowl. He was holding a dark book, and the book was bound in red satin ribbon.

He seemed embarrassed as he held it out to his cousin. 'I'm sorry, Em. I saw it, just now, on the counter.'

Mortified, Emma stood still, her eyes fixed on the book. As Mark walked towards her she backed away, shaking her head slowly from side to side.

'It won't bite you.' Mark looked surprised. 'Come on, it has to be yours.'

Aunt Peggy sighed with exasperation. 'Mark. Are you saying you didn't see who put it there?'

He turned and shrugged. 'I only left the shop for a

minute, not even that. It wasn't my fault. Sheba came in so I dragged her outside again. When I got back, the book was there.'

'But not the bringer.'

'Well, how was I to know?'

'Did you rush out to see who it was?' Aunt Peggy sounded angry.

Mark shook his head. 'No. I didn't think. Anyway, I've locked up now. Come on, Em. Open it up.'

As if in a dream, Emma stretched out her hand and took the book. Slowly she untied the ribbon, feeling a strange detachment from her actions, and then opened the green, leather-bound cover. Inside was the usual shaky inscription. 'To Emma. Hope you will be better again soon. Fondest wishes, from the lady at 99.'

'Better soon?' murmured Emma. 'But I'm not ill.'

'Hmmm, Tennyson's poems,' murmured Mark, peering over her shoulder. 'Leather-bound volume, too. Well, well. Alive or dead, I'd say the old girl's taste was improving.'

A bee hummed about Emma's face. Normally it would have sent her into a frenzy of waving arms, but now she stood motionless, staring unblinking at the book in her hand.

Mark watched her with growing concern, then snapped his fingers twice.

'Hey, wake up, little cousin. There's a marker. Turn the page and let's see what she's got marked.'

The snapping fingers caused Emma to start. She blinked several times, then opened the book to the page indicated and saw the poem, 'The May Queen'. One of the verses had been marked out lightly in pencil. Silently she stared at the words, wondering how they could relate to her.

> 'She'll find my garden-tools upon the granary floor,
> Let her take 'em: they are hers: I shall never garden
>   more:
> But tell her, when I'm gone, to train the rose-bush that
>   I set
> About the parlour-window and the box of mignonette.'

Emma's mind fled back to the cottage, and the rambling roses set on the front wall beside the window. Proof, if proof were needed, that this book really *had* come from the lady at ninety-nine. Lost in thought, she let Mark take the book from her.

He read the verse again and again, then shook his head. 'What on earth does she mean by it, whoever she is? Does she want Emma to do her gardening, or what?'

But Emma was in another world once more. She heard her aunt's distant voice and felt the firm hands about her shoulders as she was led into the house, but her own thoughts drove out the words of comfort, sending her instead into a pit of dark confusion. She stopped on the first stair, and peered back at the verse, murmuring: 'It really *is* from her. But that can't be . . . it just can't be.'

'Of course it can't. Don't let it get you down, dear,' said Aunt Peggy, urging her niece up the stairs.

'Well, it's getting me down, and that's for sure,' growled Mark. 'I'm going to the police after lunch. It's the only thing to do.'

'And tell them what?' Aunt Peggy gave him a despairing look. 'That someone is sending books to your cousin, and that you want it stopped? Whoever she is, son, she hasn't broken the law. I know, it's getting me down, too. We're all on edge these days. But we'll just have to weather it, until we find out what it's all about.'

Mark stormed up the stairs behind them. 'And *when* will that be? I'm for action now. Perhaps there's a clue in that verse.'

'I daresay there is,' said his mother. 'And when we've cleared up that little mystery, I'm sure we'll clear up the other.'

The small cemetery was tucked away behind the church on the ridge, overlooking the great vale. Large oak trees protected it from the buffeting winds of winter, but now their shadows lengthened in the golden evening sunlight and a gentle breeze soughed through the leaves, filling the churchyard with whispering.

What on earth was she doing here? Emma kept asking herself this question as she made her way to the more recent burials, at the western end of the graveyard. Was it to seek reassurance that Mrs Bennett really was dead and buried, after all? If so, then she must truly have lost her mind.

Scanning the names on each marble headstone, she came at last to a grave almost hidden beneath clumps of thistle and long grass. Reaching out, Emma pulled back the overgrowth of years and saw bold black lettering.

IN LOVING MEMORY

OF

SARAH EDITH BENNETT

WHO DIED 24TH AUGUST 1957 AGED 85 YEARS

She stared at the words for some time, until the memory of a dark shape against the sun flashed through her mind.

Glancing about her nervously, she saw, with some relief, two women tending a grave not far from her. Watching them place flowers on the neat little plot filled her with a sense of shame that no one had kept Mrs Bennett's grave tidy. She thought again of the verse in the book.

'But tell her, when I'm gone, to train the rose-bush that I set
About the parlour-window and the box of mignonette.'

Emma fell to her knees in the grass still damp from the rain, and tore out weeds by the handful. She worked hard and quickly, but even so, by the time she had plucked out the undergrowth and taken it to the large compost heap in the far corner, the sun was very low and clouds were gathering. She shivered in the cool air, and rubbed the dirt from her hands. A smell of woodsmoke filled her nostrils, mingling there with the fragrance of cut grass and laurel. She walked back to the grave and surveyed her handiwork with pride, deciding to return the following morning with fresh flowers to place before the headstone.

'There you are, Mrs Bennett,' she whispered. 'I can't train your rose-bush, but this looks much better now.'

The oak-leaves rustled above Emma as she turned and walked away.

'Two pounds of sugar, a jar of coarse-cut marmalade and half a pound of English Cheddar.' Ben's voice rang out loudly as he peered at his shopping list. 'Doris can't eat cheese of course, with her blood pressure, but I always say you can't beat a bit of Cheddar on cream crackers.'

Emma watched lazily as her aunt served Ben, and only half listened to their conversation. Not having slept for two nights, she could cheerfully have stayed in bed this morning. Instead, she had been up at six o'clock to pick flowers in the rain. Having then found an old green vase in the garden shed, she had taken this, with her bouquet, to the cemetery, filled the container with water from the wall tap there and arranged the flowers in it. They looked bright and cheerful before the headstone, but would of course fade, die and remain dead on the grave until they dissolved completely, leaving only the vase. And Emma felt somehow responsible, though she had said nothing to anyone about where she was going and had returned to the house before it was noticed that she had gone.

She felt the step ladder wobble as she climbed it to put new coffee jars on the shelf. A little help from Becky and Mark would not come amiss today, she thought grimly, but Mark was still in bed and Becky had avoided her since the third book arrived.

She's afraid, thought Emma, afraid that close proximity to the victim would increase her own chances of being caught by hobgoblins. It was an ancient belief, and it was difficult to imagine that a young girl of today could succumb to it. But then Becky surely belonged to an earlier age. Emma vaguely heard her aunt's voice:

'Well, don't forget. If there's anything either of you need, I can always send it up to you. After all, I've got an extra pair of hands now. Emma's been marvellous. I shall miss her greatly when she's gone.'

'Emma.' Ben was putting his shopping into a wicker basket as he murmured the name. He looked up thoughtfully. 'Now there's a funny thing. That was *her* name now I come to think of it.'

'Whose?' asked Aunt Peggy.

'Hers. The girl that disappeared. You remember.' He turned now and looked at Emma. 'I told you about her the other day. Emma . . . Emma . . . now what was it?' He scratched his chin and then brightened. 'Hargreaves. That was it, Emma Hargreaves.'

Aunt Peggy frowned. 'No, Ben. Her name was Elsie, surely.'

But the old man shook his head emphatically. 'No. She was Emma, I'm sure of that. She had a sister, though, if I remember correctly. Didn't they all go away after the . . . well, after the tragedy?'

Aunt Peggy leaned on an elbow and searched her memory. 'Yes, they did. I seem to recall someone telling me that they all moved to Winchester. Or was it Chichester?'

'Winchester. That was it, Winchester.'

'Did you ever hear any more of them?'

Ben shook his head. 'No, Peg. Strange business altogether. I mean to say, how can anyone vanish from the face of the earth? You'd think that after all this time someone, somewhere, would have seen or heard of the girl, alive or dead.'

Emma held the door open for him as he left. It was raining heavily now, and passing cars had their headlights full on. Mesmerized by the shining glare, she stared out through the glass panels at the wet pavement. It seemed a strange coincidence to her that the missing Emma Hargreaves was last seen outside number ninety-nine while she, Emma Morris, was supposedly receiving books from a woman who once lived there.

Aunt Peggy's voice broke through her thoughts: 'It's no use. I can't reach this top shelf. I must be shrinking with age.'

Emma turned to see her overweight aunt teetering dangerously on the step-ladder. 'Whatever are you doing?'

'Trying to clean up here.'

'But if you can't reach it properly, why use the shelf at all?'

'What, and waste good space?'

'That's better than breaking every bone in your body, surely. I'll get Mark. He's tall, and available.'

'He won't thank you,' called Aunt Peggy as Emma climbed the stairs.

Outside Mark's bedroom door Emma paused and glanced at her watch. It was half past ten. She knocked and waited. Nothing happened, although she could hear the sound of rock music from inside the room. She knocked again, this time more loudly.

'Mark. Open up, come on.'

At last the door creaked open and a dishevelled

head of blond hair appeared. Beneath it the half-closed eyes surveyed Emma sleepily. 'What's up?'

'You, I hope. It's high time, surely.'

'Hmmm?'

Emma sighed. 'Your mother could do with some help.'

'Thought you were helping.'

'I am,' replied Emma testily. 'Only I can't reach the top shelf either, and one of these days you'll come home to find *your* mother in hospital and then you'll know all about it, Mark Travis.'

With that, she swung around and marched down the stairs, leaving a bewildered youth staring after her. At the halfway landing, she heard the shop bell clang. Within seconds, it rang again. Emma entered the store just in time to see a woman in a red shiny raincoat walking out.

'Oh dear, she didn't wait.' Aunt Peggy was stepping off the ladder. 'Some people won't give you a chance, will they.'

Emma's eyes swivelled from her aunt to the counter and focused on a book bound in crimson ribbon. For one brief moment her feet were rooted to the spot, then she sprang into action, flung the door wide and dashed out into the pouring rain. She was just in time to see the red raincoat mingling in with the rest of the market day crowd.

Straining to keep her eyes on the red, Emma ran up the hill towards the square where she forced her way amid a profusion of stalls, dripping awnings and a sea of umbrellas. Keeping her quarry in sight became increasingly difficult as shoppers blocked her way. A woman wheeling a push-chair crossed her path. By the time she had found her way around mother and child, the red raincoat had vanished.

With sinking heart Emma scanned the square, searching between the stalls and ending up among the cars parked outside the Bear Hotel. Please God, please God, let her be here.

Breathless and soaked to the skin, she walked along the row of cars, peering in through the windows of each. But the only occupant was one large Alsatian dog who barked a ferocious warning at her. At length, wretched with disappointment, cold and wet, Emma began to walk back down the hill towards Travis Groceries.

'Well, at least she isn't a ghost,' she murmured to an astonished passer-by.

Aunt Peggy looked at her niece aghast as she entered the shop. 'You're soaked to the skin, child. Whatever did you mean by rushing out like that?'

'It was her,' blurted Emma. Her teeth were chattering and every muscle in her body felt taut. 'Didn't you see? She brought another one.'

'Oh yes,' said Aunt Peggy picking up the book. 'As soon as you rushed out, I saw what had happened. But even so, my dear, there was no need for you . . .'

'I almost caught her,' Emma stuttered. 'Almost . . . caught up with . . . her. She got away . . . she . . .'

'Now, you get into a nice hot bath before you catch your death,' said Aunt Peggy firmly. 'Go on, upstairs this instant!'

Mark appeared in the doorway, still pushing his shirt into denim jeans.

'Right then, where's all this work you want me to do?'

'Look.' Aunt Peggy held up the book.

Mark's eyes slipped from the book to Emma's dripping frame. 'Not another one! And what happened to you?'

Emma started shivering. 'She was in red . . . and she's . . . she's not old. She moves too . . . too quickly. I – I lost her . . . I.'

'We'll talk about it later.' Aunt Peggy took a firm hold of her niece and marched her towards the stairs. 'Look after the shop, Mark.'

But Emma resisted her aunt's attempts to pull her away, and turning to Mark, who now held the book, asked, 'What's written inside?'

'Later,' said Aunt Peggy.

'No, now.'

Mark glanced at his mother, and seeing her nod said, 'Alright. Might as well get it over with, then perhaps you'll go and dry off.' His long fingers untied the ribbon then traced the gold lettering on the dark red cover. *Helen's Choice,* he murmured. 'Well, it has to be better than *The Courage of Faith.* He turned to the fly-leaf and shrugged casually, making his voice light. 'Usual thing . . . to Emma etcetera . . .'

Something fell to the floor as he tipped the book. Bending, he saw it was a folded paper, then picked it up and handed it to his cousin.

'Looks like a note. Perhaps you'd better read it.'

Emma opened the note and saw how the creases had almost cut through the paper. Her face turned pale when she read the message it contained.

'Please come to tea on Saturday, my dear,' she read aloud. 'I shall expect you at four o'clock.'

There was a stunned silence at this, and Emma shook her head in disbelief. 'She's invited me to tea. A dead woman has invited me to tea.'

'Nonsense,' said Aunt Peggy, bustling anxiously about her niece. 'The woman who left it here wasn't dead, now was she? Up the stairs with you, and into a good hot bath. Come on!'

Emma was still staring at the note. 'Saturday. That's tomorrow.'

Mark raised his eyebrows. 'You don't mean you're taking it seriously? Oh come on, it's crazy! It has to be a joke of some sort.'

Emma stared at him and felt near to tears. 'Then who could be doing it? Who is she, this woman in red?'

They fell into a gloomy silence as Emma read and re-read the note. Then she studied the inscription on the fly-leaf of the book. 'To Emma. Fondest wishes, from the lady at ninety-nine.' Like a drowning person clutching at any straw, she clung to the notion that the clue must lie in the writing and that, if she studied it long enough, the answer would jump out at her.

As though reading her thoughts, Mark spoke. 'I've an idea. You get your bath, then we'll check this out. I know someone who might be able to tell us the identity of the writer.'

Emma smiled. 'I'll know myself, tomorrow. If I go to the cottage at four o'clock I'll know who, and why.'

'You can't be serious,' said Mark looking down at

her with deep concern on his face. 'Whoever this woman is, she's probably a fruitcake. She might even be dangerous.'

'Mark's quite right,' said Aunt Peggy, taking her niece firmly by the arm. 'You can't go swanning off by yourself to meet strangers. I want you to promise me that you won't go. Now promise.'

Before Emma could give any such pledge, however, Mark called up the stairs after her: 'I'll be waiting. We can probably solve everything before lunch.'

Chapter 7

The bookshop on the corner was small and over-
crowded. Volumes old and new were crammed on to
shelves and tables. The walls were covered with
framed maps, and the floors trampled by wet feet, as
sightseers to the town found it a useful place in which
to spend some time on a rainy day.

The owner of this literary storehouse was standing
behind a table piled high with well-thumbed
paperbacks. A tall, rather severe looking man, his
stern countenance softened as Mark and Emma
approached him. He put down the list he had been
scrutinizing and took off his horn-rimmed spectacles.

'Well now, Mark. This is a pleasant surprise. I'd
come to the conclusion that you didn't read any
more. I haven't seen you for over six months.'

Mark looked embarrassed, made pleasant conversation and introduced Emma before coming to the
reason for his visit.

'It's these books, Mr Bush,' he said, handing one
of them to the surprised bookseller. 'I was wondering if you could recall selling them to anyone recently.'

Mr Bush stared at the two beings, dressed in
kagouls, who were dripping water all over his floor,
then examined the book carefully. '*The Girlhood of
Sarah*. No, I don't recall this one. Turn of the
century, I should think. Hmmm. I do have some of

this period, and I may have sold it, but . . .' He shrugged and shook his head. 'I couldn't possibly remember.'

Emma's shoulders drooped with disappointment. Two let-downs in one day. It was all too much.

'You haven't seen a women in a red raincoat in here, have you?'

'Probably a fruitcake,' said Mark tersely.

Emma shot him a dark look. Her cousin had such a way with words.

'She might be, well, she might be just a little bit eccentric.'

Mr Bush listened with growing interest as Mark related how the books came to be in their possession, then put on his glasses once more to re-read the inscription.

At length, he shook his head and sighed. 'All I *can* tell you is that, judging by the quality of the ink, this was written many years ago. Furthermore, it was written with an old-fashioned nib, like the ones we used to use at school. I haven't seen those scratchy old things since . . . well . . . since the fifties, I should think.'

Emma stared at him in bewilderment. 'But, I don't understand. These books were sent to me only this week.'

'Maybe.' Mr Bush smiled. 'But the inscription must have been meant for another Emma. A relative, perhaps?'

'No,' murmured Emma, shaking her head. 'No. There's no one by that name.'

They thanked Mr Bush, said their farewells, and walked out into the rain, lost in their own thoughts.

Emma turned back to stare at the books displayed in the window, but her eyes fixed on nothing in particular as an ugly thought stabbed at her mind. The missing girl had been called Emma, and she used to visit the old lady. Therefore, these books must have been meant for her. There was no other explanation. Why, then, was she, Emma Morris, receiving them now from this mysterious woman in red?

Mark pulled Emma's blue hood over her head and stared down at the pale anxious face. 'Now what? You look as though you've seen a ghost.'

'Oh, funny.' Emma smiled wryly, then shuddered. 'But I do feel that someone has just walked over my grave. I'm frightened, Mark. What's happening?'

'Nothing to get alarmed about.'

Mark's voice was reassuring and, as he zipped up his jacket, Emma searched his face for guidance. All she saw, however, was confusion. Still, she thought, at least he was here, and his presence was a great comfort.

A suspicion had taken root in her mind and she wondered how he would react to it. At last she spoke it aloud.

'Do you think Mary Ann's behind all this?'

'Mary Ann? Why?'

'Because no one else knows me. She's an odd person, odd enough to do anything. After all, she warned me to leave, said I was in danger.'

'Only she wouldn't tell you what she'd seen in the leaves.'

Emma shook her head. 'I'm wondering if *she* isn't trying to make me leave for some reason.'

'What reason?'

'I don't know. I just wondered if you could think of anything. What do you know of her?'

Mark stared at his cousin with furrowed brow. 'Only what I've told you. She's ignorant and superstitious, but clever with herbs. People like Mary Ann used to be burned as witches. She wouldn't harm a soul, though. I can't believe she'd want to do anything like this.'

'I've just remembered something Becky once said,' Emma murmured. 'She said that Mary Ann knew the missing girl. How could I have forgotten that? Mary Ann knew Emma Hargreaves. Mark, I think we should have a talk with her, really I do.'

Snug against the rain, Mary Ann's cottage looked inviting as Mark and Emma trudged through the wet field towards its stone walls. Smoke spiralled upwards from the chimney, only to be sent billowing back by the willow trees to drift, veil-like, over the thatched roof.

They must have been seen from the window for suddenly the front door opened and Mary Ann stood there, holding the ginger cat close to her shoulder.

Mark waved as they approached. 'Hi there. How are you?'

'How am I?' Mary Ann looked haughty. 'That's a strange question from you, Mark Travis, seeing as how I never see you from one month to the next. What brings you here now?'

Mark held up a plastic shopping bag, heavy with books. 'We'd like your help, if you've time to spare.'

Mary Ann looked from the bag to Emma. 'I do

hope you still wear that angelica, child. You know what I told you.'

She led the way into the cottage and bade Emma sit down in the chair beside the fire.

'Now, then.'

Emma took the bag from Mark, unzipped it and brought out one of the books.

'This came for me the other day. I wondered if you had ever seen it before?'

Bewildered, Mary Ann took the book, opened it, then frowned as she read the inscription. 'From the lady at 99.' She sank down on the chair opposite to Emma murmuring, 'Why that's . . . that's . . .'

'Mrs Bennett,' murmured Emma helpfully.

Mary Ann looked at her sharply. 'Where did you get this?'

'It just came,' answered Emma, feeling the warmth from the fire against her wet jeans.

'In the post?'

'No. It was put on the shop counter.'

Emma stared hard at Mary Ann for the slightest glimmer of nervousness or guilt. But there was only puzzlement in those strange, colourless eyes.

'But who put it there?'

'That's what we're trying to find out,' said Mark.

Mary Ann set her head on one side like a bird eyeing a worm. 'You think I had something to do with it?'

'Oh no,' said Emma quickly. 'It's just that we'd be glad of any information you could throw to us, since you once knew the girl who vanished . . .'

'You think these books were for her?' Mary Ann handed back the book. Immediately, Emma gave her the Tennyson, which she took in some surprise, then she leaned back in a relaxed fashion and opened it. The ginger cat jumped on to her lap, turned around three times and settled into a sleeping position with its nose buried in its soft fur. A loud purring filled the room.

Emma watched Mary Ann carefully, saw the faint start of recognition as she read the poem, and let a dark thought take root. This woman was about the same height and build as the woman in the red raincoat. Only the hair left room for doubt. She had barely seen more than the back of the mysterious messenger, but nevertheless her earlier suspicions were growing.

'The May Queen.' Mary Ann almost whispered this to herself as she stared at the book. 'I remember.'

Mark looked surprised. 'Remember? Remember what, exactly?'

'She told me, Emma told me.' Her voice seemed far away, as Mary Ann's thoughts slipped back to childhood days. 'She was ill. I can't remember what it was, though. I went to see her and as I sat on her bed she showed me this book. It came from an old lady she used to visit. The lady loved her garden, and Emma used to help her in it. When I asked why this . . . this . . .'

'Mrs Bennett,' Emma repeated.

'. . . this Mrs Bennett had marked out the verse, Emma replied that "her lady", that's what she called the old woman, that "her lady" had asked her to care for the garden when she was gone from this world. Emma had promised that she would, until such time as someone else bought the cottage.' Mary Ann's face clouded over. 'But who could have dreamed then that Emma would go before the old lady? Do you know, on the very day she disappeared she was going to have tea at the cottage. I remember that, because she showed me the note. She'd received it the day before, inside a book.'

'An invitation to tea?' Emma felt the colour drain from her face and glanced uneasily at Mark, who was seated beside the cluttered table.

'We went shopping that morning,' Mary Ann went on, 'and Emma bought some roses. Apparently the old lady was very fond of roses.' She paused, looked across at Emma and frowned. 'You look a lot like Emma Hargreaves, you know. I thought that, as soon as I saw you, and I knew then that . . . that you were destined to suffer the same fate.'

Emma felt sick with fear. 'What fate? What did you see in the leaves, Mary Ann?'

'I'd rather not say.'

'But you *must* say.' Emma's voice was shrill as hysteria rose within her. 'Why is my fate the same as hers? What did you see?'

Mark rushed to his cousin's side and put a protective arm about her. 'Don't let her get to you. It's all nonsense, you know it is.' He stared at Mary Ann angrily. 'What do you think you're doing, frightening Emma like that?'

Mary Ann put down the cat and quickly stood up. 'I'm only trying to warn her, but she won't listen. I told her to leave Athelbury.'

'But she *can't* leave Athelbury, and you know it!'

snapped Mark. 'Anyway, what has all this got to do with the books we asked about?'

Mary Ann folded her arms and sighed deeply. 'I don't know, and that's the honest truth. All I do know is what I saw.'

'*What* did you see?' cried Emma.

Mary Ann walked across to the window and stared out at the falling rain. It was some time before she spoke.

'I saw you in a terrible place, a dark and cold place.'

Mark's arm tightened on Emma's trembling frame. 'What is this place?'

'I can't tell. But she's not alone, Emma Hargreaves is there too. Ask the gipsies. They'll know alright. As to the books,' Mary Ann swung around and stared at Emma 'it must be that she is trying to warn you herself.'

Emma's eyes opened wider. 'Emma Hargreaves? You mean you think she's still alive? Of course! What other explanation can there be? She's still alive.'

But Mary Ann shook her head. 'I said no such thing. I said she was trying to warn you. I believe her warning comes from beyond the grave.'

'Tosh,' said Mark, trying to force a laugh. 'If Emma's sending books, then Emma's alive and well and living in Athelbury.'

Outside once more, Mark shouted above the noise of rain and ducks as they walked past the village pond.

'No wonder Becky's so impossible these days. Who wouldn't be, after a spell in there? We'll have to stop her visiting Mary Ann. Did you see the books the woman reads?'

Still badly shaken by Mary Ann's words, Emma slowed her pace and stood staring across the pond in a glazed and vacant manner. 'Do you . . . do you think there's anything in what she said? Do you think that Emma Hargreaves *is* trying to contact me from beyond the grave?'

'Rubbish,' said Mark angrily. 'If Emma Hargreaves is trying to contact you, and goodness knows why, then she's certainly not dead.'

Emma turned and stared up at him, feeling the soft rain in her face. 'But Mary Ann said . . .'

'Mary Ann's nuts! The whole thing's nuts, if you ask me. What are you to Emma Hargreaves, anyway? You don't even live here. I tell you, the whole thing's crazy. Maybe *she's* crazy, maybe she did go off with the gipsies after all, and it turned her mind. I don't know.'

The Raggle Taggle Gipsies! Emma's thoughts fled back to the cottage and the singer. Could it have been Emma Hargreaves? If so, why was she hiding? Why not show herself to people and clear up an age-old mystery? Mark was right. Why would she take an interest in a girl from London, who just happened to resemble her when young? After all, Emma Hargreaves would be about forty years old now. She started walking on.

'But this terrible place Mary Ann spoke about. What did you make of all that, Mark?'

Mark looked down at her and smiled. 'Amateur dramatics. She says things like that to gain attention and notoriety. It's all she has left. No marriage, no children, no career, after years of looking after her sick father. It's a lifeline to her, I suppose.'

They walked on in silence and Emma tried to pretend she had not been badly frightened by Mary Ann, but she failed so miserably that Mark could sense her fear.

'Don't worry, Em. We'll go to the police and show them the books.' He was breathless as they climbed the steep cobbled hill once more. 'After all, they must count as evidence in a case that was never closed.'

'We'd be laughing stocks,' said Emma. 'What are we going to say? We can hardly tell them that a woman who died twenty five years ago is sending me books. They would just laugh and tell us to find the joker.'

'It's not so funny at that,' said Mark. 'It could yield up Emma Hargreaves's whereabouts.'

His cousin listened, as he talked, but her own thoughts took over once again. Maybe that other Emma was alive, or maybe she was dead. Maybe Mary Ann was right, and some horror was awaiting her. Well, whatever the outcome, the answer would be there for her at four o'clock the following day when she answered the strange invitation, just as Emma Hargreaves had so many years ago.

Emma looked at her watch. It was half past four. This time tomorrow, she thought, she would know just who was behind all this, and why.

Sleep was out of the question that night. Emma lay tossing and turning, her mind in a turmoil, her body a mass of tense nerves. Not until the eastern sky turned to grey did she drift into uneasy slumbers that brought ugly dreams.

She found herself back in the High Street and there, ahead, the woman in red walked quickly among the many shoppers. Emma was running after her, but her legs became too heavy, and for all her effort it seemed she moved in slow motion. She tried to push away the people crowding in on both sides, but they were too strong and just started laughing.

Suddenly, she was in the Market Square and gaining slowly on the mysterious figure. The woman had stopped with her back turned to Emma, who kept her eyes on the red raincoat until it seemed that her whole vision was filled with the colour red. Then the figure began to turn. Emma reeled back and found herself staring up at a black silhouette against the bright sun.

A shout broke through her dream. She shot up in bed, her heart pounding against her ribs, her body soaked in sweat. Slowly, as reason returned, Emma realized that the cry had been her own.

A dream, she murmured, just a bad dream. She settled back under the covers and lay there feeling badly frightened. Had it been another warning? The woman in red seemed to say, 'Follow me,' but the figure against the sun said, 'Go back.'

One had been real, but what of the other?

'Are my cricket whites ready, Mum?' Mark walked into the dining room where his mother was ladling out tomato soup into four bowls. 'I can't find them anywhere.'

'Look in the airing cupboard,' said Aunt Peggy. 'I

didn't think you'd be playing after all that rain. The ground must be soaked.'

Mark glanced out of the window. 'Oh, I don't know. It's hotting up again. The grass should dry out in no time.'

Lunch was a mainly silent affair and to Emma, tense and nervous, it seemed that everyone knew what she was about to do. They would surely band together and bar her way, just as the crowd had barred her way in the dream last night. She prayed that no mention would be made of the invitation to tea.

Mark had been a staunch ally and, at her insistance, had said nothing to his mother and sister of their visit to Mary Ann's cottage. Emma glanced at him across the table, glad that he was now preoccupied with the coming cricket match: otherwise, he would certainly have stopped her. Her eyes drifted towards Becky, but those icy orbs refused to look up to meet her gaze. Emma smiled to herself. Slipping away this afternoon might prove easy enough after all.

'Are you riding today?' Aunt Peggy was looking at her daughter.

Becky nodded, broke off a piece of roll and buttered it. 'Hmm, the ride's booked for three o'clock.'

'You're taking Emma with you, I trust?'

Becky almost choked on the roll, and Emma seized her opportunity.

'No, no, Aunty, I'd rather stay here, if you don't mind. I'm pretty tired. Didn't sleep very well last night.'

'Oh dear, I'm sorry to hear that. Still, I think you'll enjoy it at the riding stables. Becky will take you, *won't* you! Becky!'

The 'won't you' spoke volumes. It meant: 'Keep an eye on Emma even if you have to tie her up.'

'She won't get a ride,' Becky was saying. 'They're all booked. Honey's been sold and Candy's gone lame, so they're two ponies short anyway.'

'That doesn't matter,' said Aunt Peggy. 'She can watch you.'

What she really means, thought Emma, is that Becky must watch *me*. Her heart sank. Slipping away was not going to be so easy. She tried again.

'I'd be just as happy in the garden with a good book, honest I would.'

'Nonsense.' Aunt Peggy's tone did not invite argument. 'Becky would love to take you along.'

So, then, it was settled. Becky was to watch her like a hawk in case she had a mind to go wandering into dangerous places.

By three o'clock the August weather had settled back to normal again, and it was hot in the vale. The smell of stables, horses and turf crowded in on Emma as she leaned over the neat white fence of Merrifield Farm and watched the riders in the paddock.

Becky looked good on her chestnut mare. The pony was frisky, though, giving her rider a hard time as she tried to pace her for the jumps. But they cleared them without mishap, and returned to their place in the line.

Watching one rider after another jump was like

98

counting sheep, and Emma began to yawn sleepily. Becky twisted in her saddle to keep a wary eye on her, and there seemed no possibility of escape. She looked at her watch anxiously. The hands stood at a quarter past three. She had already noticed how the lane wound its way uphill, past Swallow Field and on into town. It would take about twenty minutes to the Market Square, she thought. If she failed to make her getaway soon, it would be too late.

The class of young equestrians soldiered on, and Emma began to despair. She put her hand in the pocket of her blouse and felt her fingers close over the wilting angelica stem. Becky had found it on the coffee table and put it by her pillow. Seeing it there had sent floods of relief through Emma, although now she wondered just how a dying herb could ward off danger.

One of the instructors was walking away from the class. She opened a gate on the far side of the paddock, then called out an order which Emma could not hear. At once, the riders trotted out into the field beyond, then urged their mounts to a canter.

Emma stiffened as they headed for the woods. At long last they were off on a ride, and she was free. She saw Becky looking back anxiously, and gave a reassuring wave to her cousin. But no sooner had the class ridden out of sight than Emma struck out for the lane, to keep the strangest appointment of her life.

Chapter 8

The lane was deserted as Emma approached the cottage. She had run past Swallow Field in fear, hurried up the steep hill and slipped past the cricket field where Mark, fielding at Square Leg with his eyes firmly on the batsman, had failed to see her go by. Only little Tommy, watching the match from his favourite perch on the fence, noticed her and gave a friendly wave.

At the gate Emma paused, hot, watchful and tense, hoping that whoever had invited her here would be in the garden and waiting. She could see no one about, and scanned the windows for any sign of movement.

'Is anyone there?' she called.

There was no sound, and no movement of any kind. Her eyes went up to the windows once more. Someone *was* in there, she was certain of it. Someone was inside the cottage, and watching her every move. Nervous at the thought, Emma felt for the angelica in her pocket. It was still there, but she took little comfort from it now.

'Hello in there!' she called again. 'Is anyone about?'

Too on edge to stand still for long, Emma squeezed through the gate and moved forward slowly, her eyes glued to the windows. This time, she thought, safety was best served by staying out in the open. Let this woman, whoever she was, come out to face her in broad daylight. It was high time that she did.

Tentatively, she inched her way along the path, then stepped into the long grass to her right and across the overgrown lawn. In the shade of the chestnut tree she glanced at her watch and decided to give the mystery lady no more than ten minutes. After that, she would return to the shop.

She was starting to examine the rambling rose which trailed by the window, when she heard a movement in the briars behind her and swung around in fear.

'Who's there?'

Silence greeted her words. A bird, she thought, letting her shoulders fall. Then the briars rustled again and Emma felt the hairs on her neck shoot upright.

'Who is it? Who's there?'

Still no answer. Rooted to the spot, her eyes fixed on the bushes, Emma felt panic overtaking her. If only someone would walk along the lane, she thought. What a little fool she had been coming here alone! Mark had warned her, Mary Ann had warned her. Fool! Why had she not listened?

She started as the bushes moved again, then frowned with suspicion.

'Emma! Is it you, Emma Hargreaves?' As the thought took hold, she moved forward slightly. 'Why do you hide from me? There's no need. Why do you send me books? Why did you let people think you were . . .?'

Her words turned to a gasp as the bushes parted and the gipsy boy jumped out. Shocked at his sudden appearance, Emma staggered backwards, felt her feet hit against something hard, then tripped. Her hands clawed the air frantically, but where ground should have been there was nothing. With appalling suddenness, she was engulfed in darkness; falling, screaming and twisting. Then her shoulder hit something hard; her flailing hands caught rope, and burned as they slid down it. Her body gave a violent jerk, and she was swinging in space.

Dazed and shocked, she swung there, unable to think what had happened. Her hands tightened on the rope. There was a clatter from below her, followed by a faint and distant thud. Horror swept over her as realization dawned. She must be in a well; she was hanging for her very life.

Panic took hold. Emma wanted to thrash about like a stranded fish, but instinct told her that survival depended on stillness.

Her hands were slipping, her shoulders were shot through with pain. She tried to get a firmer grip on the rope, wondering in terror how strong it was. How long could she hang like this? How long before the rope gave way under her weight? Surely it must be rotten with damp and age.

A piercing scream echoed round the narrow tunnel, a sound of unspeakable terror, a sound she never knew she had made. Then:

'No need for panic.' The voice was a distant echo.

Emma raised her head and saw a face appear in the small circle of light high above her.

'Help me, please help me.'

'You 'ang on there, now. I'll try and pull the rope up.'

'It's going to break,' screamed Emma. 'Get help! Get more rope. Please, oh, please help me.' She felt a tug on the rope and knew she was moving slowly upwards, then suddenly the line slackened and she felt herself spinning crazily. Terrified, she clung more tightly.

'No, don't. It's no use.' Her screams echoed around her head. 'I can't hang on much longer.'

'You can. You *must*.' The face gazed down, and the voice, so full of concern, was young; too young, thought Emma, fearing it would be the last voice she ever heard. Even if Eddy wanted to help her after the way he had been treated, he would not be able to do it alone. 'I need more rope.'

'In the shed!' screamed Emma 'But don't leave me alone. Don't leave me!'

The face disappeared and light shone down once more. Emma swung there, the strain on her arms and shoulders growing almost unbearable, and gave herself up to despair. At last, she heard another voice.

'It's me, Em. Don't worry. We'll get you out, so hang in there.'

She heard in disbelief. 'Mark? Is it you, Mark?' She told herself that she was dreaming. Eddy had run away and left her, and she was hallucinating before falling to her death.

'Now listen carefully. The wynch has gone, and this rope's badly worn, so I'm lowering Eddy on another rope. Grab hold of him and the new rope, and I'll pull you both up.'

Emma heard him but shook her head in despair. 'You can't. We'll be too heavy.'

Coldness and pain were taking their toll now and a great weariness overwhelmed her. It was silent, as silent as the grave. Soon, this hideous place would be her grave, she thought, and she heard again Mary Ann's words: ' . . . I saw you in a terrible place, a dark and cold place . . .' She looked up. Two feet were dangling above her. Then she became aware of something flapping in front of her face. It was the tail end of the rope tied about the gipsy boy. She saw him twist until his feet touched the walls then, wedged between the sides of the well, he slowly lowered himself until he was able to get an arm around Emma's waist.

'Grab on, girl. Grab the rope.'

In spite of his arm, Emma was loathe to let go of her lifeline.

'Come on. Get your 'ands across. I've got you. I won't let you fall, but be quick about it.'

With a supreme effort, Emma forced herself to let go with her left hand, caught the other rope, then brought her right hand across. With the boy's arm firmly about her waist, she felt them both moving upwards and marvelled at Mark's strength in lifting the two of them. Something dropped past them and disappeared in the darkness below.

'That was the rope,' she cried. 'It's gone.'

The circle of light grew larger as they drew towards the mouth of the well. She kept her eyes fixed on it, praying silently. Suddenly, a dark shape appeared against the bright sun. Emma stared in horror, knowing she had seen it twice before, once in the garden and once in a dream. Had it been a warning after all? Then it was gone, leaving a shaft of sunlight stabbing down at them.

They were at the rim now, and could feel the warm sun on their faces. Emma climbed out ahead of Eddy, who pushed her upwards, then turned to help him. Only when he, too, was safe did she succumb to exhaustion. Sinking to her knees, sobbing with relief and shock, she looked up at the boy who had saved her life by risking his own; but he was already on his feet and moving nervously away.

'I meant no 'arm, girl. It were them berries I come for. You 'ad no cause to fear me like that.'

Kneeling there in the cool grass, Emma stared up at him through her tears. 'You saved my life. I can't thank you enough.'

Eddy was untying the rope from his waist and Emma let her eyes follow the line. It led to Mark, standing in his cricket whites with the coil about him still and the rest of the rope firmly anchored to the trunk of the tree. Red faced and panting from effort, Mark moved anxiously towards his cousin.

'Are you alright?'

Emma nodded, felt tears flooding her eyes once more, and was unable to stop her body from trembling. Her shoulder hurt badly; but she was alive, and that was a miracle. Had it not been for the gipsy boy and Mark, then she would, by now, have fallen to her death. She stared up at her cousin in growing bewilderment.

'But what are you doing here? You were playing cricket.'

Mark released himself from the rope, flung it to

the ground and frowned. 'It was strange. Do you know that little boy called Tommy?'

Emma nodded. 'Yes. He was watching you play just now.'

'That's right. But suddenly he came chasing across the wicket shouting his head off. I caught him and asked him "what the devil he thought he was doing?" He said that the lady had told him to get help because Emma was in danger. I followed him, and he led me here. Then I told him to run across to Ben for help.'

Emma was looking at him strangely. 'Which lady?'

Mark shrugged. 'When I got here, I only saw Eddy.'

At that moment Ben came shuffling through the gate. He looked puffed and worried.

'I've called the police,' he shouted, 'and the ambulance, and the fire brigade. What's happened? Is anyone hurt?'

Mark led the old man over to the well and told him what had happened. Ben turned swiftly to little Tommy who had been following him, and sent him to stand beside the gate.

'This is no place for a child. God in heaven, when I think of all those nippers coming in here, and all the time this was . . .' He broke off as words failed.

While the rest of the small group talked together, Emma kept staring down at the terrifying hole that had nearly swallowed her up forever. Slowly her eyes became accustomed to the darkness, and she peered more closely.

'There's something down there.'

Mark and Eddy gathered close about her but

neither could make anything out. They decided she was just imagining things.

'But there *is* something,' Emma persisted. 'It's something light. Mind you, I heard the pail go down just after I fell. Maybe it's that.'

She looked up and saw Eddy's frightened face. He was staring at the road, murmuring, 'They'll say it was my fault. They'll say I pushed you.'

Emma turned her head, saw the white police car drawing into the kerb and turned back to the gipsy boy.

'Of course they won't, Eddy. I'm going to tell them how you and Mark saved my life. Come back, please come back. You've nothing to be afraid about.'

But the gipsy boy had already dashed through the hedge and was legging it down the steep hillside to Swallow Field.

There was no time to chase after him, since two policemen were now approaching the group at the well-head. Because of the heat they had left their jackets in the car and now wore the sleeves of their blue shirts rolled up to the elbows. One pushed back his cap as he stared down the well, whistled slowly, then murmured to his colleague.

'It's like the one at Donning Ridge. Do you remember? Still, no one fell down that one. Now then, Miss. Can you tell us what happened?'

In faltering tones Emma explained that she had tripped, fallen, and caught the rope. She told them about Eddy, the gipsy boy, and praised her cousin too, for saving her life. To their concerned questions, she assured them that she was not hurt.

'Well, you shouldn't go playing in here,' one policeman said. 'Old property can be dangerous. You'd be surprised how many kids get hurt this way.'

'What, by falling down wells?' Mark looked surprised.

'Oh, no. Mind you, considering how many wells were sunk in Athelbury, we've been pretty lucky there. Most of them are filled in now, though. We didn't know about this one.'

Then they wanted to know how Mark had managed to save his cousin. How had he known where she was?

'The little boy told me that some woman had sent him to fetch help.'

'I see.' The policeman was writing in his notebook. 'And where is this woman now?'

'There!' Emma's shrill voice cut the air, as she pointed towards the lane.

Mark turned, and saw a woman in a red plastic raincoat standing across the road, staring at them.

'Is that the woman who brought the book, Em?'

But Emma was already halfway down the garden path. The woman in red turned and walked along the street with small, scuffling, movements that seemed to give her the speed and motion of a rodent.

'Come back,' cried the policeman after Emma. 'I haven't finished taking your statement.'

'We'll be back,' said Mark, sprinting through the gate after his cousin.

Passing Emma in the lane, he turned the bend, only to find the woman had gone. The fire engine drove past, at speed, its siren blaring.

Breathless, Emma came alongside him. 'I don't

believe it,' she gasped. 'She couldn't just vanish like that.'

Mark paused and stood with his hands on his hips, shaking his head in disbelief.

'She didn't seem to be travelling that fast. Still, she isn't Mary Ann, and she certainly isn't a ghost.'

'Then who is she?'

'Who else could she be,' murmured Mark, 'but Emma Hargreaves?'

'Then she must be the one who warned Tommy.'

'I'll bet she's cut through to the swing park,' said Mark. 'There's no other way she could have gone from here.'

Following her cousin into a narrow alleyway that stretched between the cottages towards the vale, Emma could see the small swing park ahead of her. There were several children playing on the slide, and a young mother was pushing a toddler on the baby swing; but Emma's eyes were drawn instantly to the bench at the edge of the ridge.

The lady in red sat there, her back to Emma and Mark, her face staring out over the vale. As they approached quietly they could hear her humming, then the humming broke into low song. The sound made Emma's flesh creep once more.

> 'Last night you slept on a goose-feather bed,
> With the sheet turned down so bravely O,
>
> Tonight you'll sleep in an open field,
> Along with the raggle-taggle gipsies O.'

As she sang the woman rocked to and fro in a doll-like movement and was oblivious to Mark as he

109

walked slowly around the side of the bench to confront her.

Emma made to move forward, but Mark's hand raised in warning made her pause. Now what had he in mind? She stared back at the woman and saw how the mouse-coloured hair hung straight and was unevenly cut, the right side longer than the left, and was clipped back with a large pink plastic slide. Thin and tense, she seemed like a little animal sniffing the air for danger. Moving around to her side, Emma took in the narrow pinched face, pale and plain, an ageless face that could have been twenty or fifty years old.

Ben had said that Emma Hargreaves was pretty, she seemed to remember. This woman was anything but, and even as a child must have had the same pinched features. She saw Mark smiling down at the woman in a friendly manner.

'Hello. Thanks for sending the little boy to me. My cousin's alright now. How did you know she was in danger, though?

She looked up at him sharply, stiffened and clutched a black plastic handbag close to her.

'Go away. I don't know you,' she snapped in a high, childlike voice. Mark decided to change course and came to the point bluntly. 'You sent books to Emma, didn't you? Why?'

The head moved like a startled mouse. 'Because they belong to her, that's why. I don't know you. Who are you?'

'I'm Emma's cousin.'

'Nonsense. We have no cousins.'

Mark shot a bewildered glance in Emma's direction.

'No, Emma's *my* cousin, and she's been receiving books from you. But she doesn't know who you are.'

'She knows me, alright. She's just pretending. Emma's always pretending. It's her way of teasing. It's her way of paying me back.'

'Paying you back for what?' asked Mark; but the woman had started rocking backwards and forwards in time to the tune she was humming and seemed to hear him no longer.

Realizing she was sick in her mind he stood quietly, wondering if there was anything to be gained by talking to her. Suddenly she stopped humming and stared up at him in a questioning manner.

'It wasn't my fault, anyway. Why should she have all the fun? Why always Emma and not me? I never got one single invitation, not one. It just wasn't fair.'

Mark caught his cousin's eye and frowned. Slowly, a thought entered his head, something he had never before considered. But first he had to make sure.

'You're *not* Emma Hargreaves,' he murmured.

The pinched face looked up, shadowed with sadness.

'Emma went with the gipsies, just like the fine lady in the song. They came and took her away.'

'Then who are you?'

'I'm her sister, Elsie.'

Mark stared across at Emma and saw her make as if to move forward. He stopped her with a quick gesture. Whatever had happened to Elsie had caused her mind to stay trapped in the past. She seemed to think her sister was here, in Athelbury, and that she took the form of his cousin. But why? What on earth had happened to make her believe such a thing? He

111

searched his mind for the right thing to say. At last he found it.

'Your sister used to visit the old lady at number ninety-nine, didn't she?'

Elsie snorted. '*I* was never invited, though. No one ever invites me anywhere. But then, Emma's pretty, and I'm not. The last time she went to tea, I made certain that I went too.' She slammed her handbag down on to her lap, then started rocking to and fro once more as her face clouded over. 'But Emma got angry with me. At the gate, she tried to make me go back. We had a fight. I hated her then. I wanted to hurt her. But she ran into the garden laughing . . . laughing . . . laughing . . .' The voice broke off, and the rocking stopped. 'Then she was gone.'

'Gone?'

Elsie nodded. 'They can do that, you know. The gipsies can make you vanish. I kept calling her name. I got frightened and told her I was sorry. If she came back, I wouldn't stay. I would go home and behave. I went home, but Emma stayed with the gipsies. We had to go away after that.'

Standing behind Elsie, Emma felt faintness sweep over her; and she heard again Mary Ann's words: 'But she's not alone. Emma Hargreaves is there, too.' Of course. The faint bundle lying at the bottom of the well was her luckless namesake, and no one, not even her little sister, had dreamed that Emma Hargreaves was still at number ninety-nine.

This same thought had occurred to Mark, who was now staring at Elsie in horror.

'But didn't you tell anyone about Emma?'

The sad and lost surviving sister shook her head forlornly. 'How could I tell anyone? They would punish me for fighting. We're not allowed to fight, you see.'

Mark knelt down beside the woman and smiled with sympathetic understanding. 'And why have you returned to Athelbury, Elsie?'

'To find her,' came the faint reply. 'And I did. She's left the gipsies now, because I saw her in the shop. I heard her say that it was going to be her birthday, so I brought back one of the books, hoping she would remember me.' Elsie's hand tightened on the handbag. 'I kept those books, you see, and I know they mean a lot to her. I wanted to give them back. I thought she would be pleased. But she pretends not to know me.'

Emma gripped the back of the seat to steady herself. The dreadful accident to her namesake had clearly turned Elsie's mind. To her, Emma Hargreaves was still alive, thirteen years of age, and helping in a shop. Mark had been remarkably quick-thinking to prevent Elsie from coming face to face with the real live Emma Morris. Such a confrontation might well have shattered the woman's happy illusion that her sister was well, and send her plummeting into real madness. She must never know the truth, never know that twenty-five years had passed and that her sister's bones lay at the bottom of a dark, dank well.

Mark's voice was kind and soft. 'Did you know there was an invitation to tea still inside one of the books?'

Elsie nodded her mouselike head. 'Oh, I wasn't

going to push in this time. I just wanted to see her. Only . . . only . . . I was afraid she would laugh at me, like she always did. So I just watched her. Then she was gone again, like before.' The pinched face clouded momentarily, then cleared as a pleasant thought entered that confused mind. 'But this time, she *did* come back.'

'Then why didn't you go over to see her?' asked Mark.

'No. I couldn't do that. You see, she's still angry with me. I don't think she'll ever be my friend again.'

Elsie Hargreaves bent her head and two large tears ran down her pale cheeks.

Chapter 9

In a matter of hours news of the accident had swept through Athelbury, and a crowd soon gathered outside number ninety-nine to watch as police and firemen finally brought Emma Hargreaves out of the well. Shocked and deeply saddened, people searched their memories, and anger that had for so long been directed at the gipsies was now suddenly turned on the town council.

'It's a disgrace. They should have had that well filled in years ago.'

'They must have known about it. If not, why not?'

'It's a wonder that other children didn't fall in.'

'I always thought there was something sinister about this cottage.'

Unaware of the angry emotions she had unleashed, Emma awoke on the Sunday morning to the sweet sound of church bells and stretched out lazily in her bed. She was still very tired, having suffered another sleepless night, and her shoulder muscles hurt whenever she moved; but she was alive, and that was all that mattered.

Marvelling at her miraculous escape, Emma twisted her head, looked through the window at the hazy blue sky and let her thoughts turn to the gipsy boy who had helped her. He must be thanked properly, she thought, and everyone in Athelbury must know how he had risked his life to save her.

She sighed and bit her bottom lip thoughtfully, wondering what had happened to poor Elsie Hargreaves. So much for ghosts! It seemed incredible now that she had been brought close to believing in them. But that was Becky's fault, surely. Well, maybe now she, too, would come to her senses and pay less heed to Mary Ann's rantings. Emma frowned as she faced an unpalatable truth, for it had to be said of Mary Ann that she had been spot on in her predictions.

There was a gentle tap on the bedroom door, it creaked open and Aunt Peggy put her head into the room. 'Thought you might still be sleeping. How do you feel, dear?'

Emma raised herself up on one elbow, felt a pain shoot through her shoulder and lay back once more. 'My shoulders hurt, but otherwise I'm fine.'

Aunt Peggy smiled. 'Fancy a cup of tea?'

'No thanks. I'm getting up now and going out into the sunshine.' Emma frowned. 'Do you know, Aunty, I thought . . . I thought I would never see it again. I thought I would fall, and perhaps not be killed outright but lie there injured for days and days in darkness, and no one knowing I was there. Just as she did.'

'Now then, now then.' Aunt Peggy advanced towards her niece, sat down on the bed and stroked Emma's forehead lovingly. 'It's all over now, and you're safe. But the doctor said you were to rest in bed this morning.'

'But I . . .'

'No buts. Those muscles won't mend unless they're rested.'

'I must go to Swallow Field, though. I must thank Eddy. Do you think Mark would come with me?'

'Of course. In fact, we'll all come with you.' Aunt Peggy smiled. 'I say *we*, but I'm still not so sure about Becky. She's been very quiet these past few hours. I think she's pretty shocked at what happened. But she'll come round, eventually.'

Emma was silent. She didn't want Becky to go to Swallow Field, for having been on the receiving end of her silent hostility, she had no wish to inflict it on others. Anyway, she thought, Eddy's heroic act would not change overnight the prejudice that was so deeply ingrained.

'Do you know that the phone hasn't stopped ringing,' said Aunt Peggy. 'It drove me mad last night, and started again at seven o'clock this morning. Fancy ringing people up at that hour on a Sunday.'

'Who's been ringing, then?'

'Oh, newspaper people, friends and so on. News like that travels pretty fast.' Aunt Peggy frowned. 'I still can't believe that we nearly lost you. All night I've thought of it. What your father will say, I just don't know.'

Emma realized suddenly how tired her aunt looked. 'There's no need to tell him. It's all over now.'

Aunt Peggy sighed and shook her head sadly. 'That poor girl. All those years . . . poor, poor creature. And that sister of hers, well I mean to say, fancy her not going for help. What can she have been thinking of?'

'She didn't understand what had happened,' said

117

Emma. 'She was very young at the time.' Her mind slipped back to that moment in the swing park when Elsie Hargreaves had wept for her sister. Emma had been very careful not to reveal herself to the poor demented woman, and even when the police arrived on the scene had kept well in the background.

'They're taking her back to Winchester, I hear,' said Aunt Peggy. 'Apparently she's been in a home for the mentally frail since her parents died. She just walked out about two weeks ago, and no one knew where to look for her. She's been at large all that time.'

'At large,' Emma laughed. 'Oh, Aunty! She's not a criminal.'

'I know, I know, but when I think how she got you in her sights it makes my flesh creep, really it does.'

'Why? She's harmless enough, and she meant no harm. She thought I was her sister, that's all. She returned here especially to look for Emma, and that's why she brought the books back. It was her way of making atonement, I think. And she must never be told that her sister is dead. It would be too cruel.'

'Now don't you go fretting about that. The doctors know all about these things. Still, if she didn't mean to harm you, why lure you to that garden in the first place?'

'Because it's where she last saw her sister.' Emma tried to sit up once more, and this time was successful. 'Anyway, as soon as she realized I was in danger she sent Tommy for help. Thank goodness Mark was playing cricket. At least he didn't have to look too far.'

At that point a disturbing thought crossed Emma's mind. If Elsie Hargreaves had not known about the well, why then should she suddenly have become so alarmed?

'Well now, how about bacon and eggs?' Aunt Peggy's voice was brisk and meant to jog Emma out of the reverie she had fallen into. 'I can throw in some fried bread and tomatoes.'

Emma suddenly felt very hungry. 'Hmmm, yes please.'

But as Aunt Peggy left the room, she pondered again the question that was pricking at her mind. Why had Elsie sent Tommy for help if she didn't know of the danger? Slowly, she got out of bed, walked across to the window and looked out. The High Street was quiet, the sun was shining and the church bells were sweet music. It was good to be alive.

As she stood at the window, it slowly began to dawn on her that Elsie Hargreaves *did* know. Somewhere, deep inside that troubled mind, was locked a truth so terrible that nature had wrapped it away from consciousness, protecting Elsie as a mother protects her child from the cold. Maybe the little girl had rushed to where her sister disappeared, seen the yawning hole and found the guilt and horror of that moment too much to bear. Better, then, to block out the scene; block out the passing years, too, so that Emma Hargreaves was still thirteen years of age and playing a silly prank.

Emma turned and looked at her pale reflection in the mirror. Was it little mischievous Elsie, then, who had started the rumour about the gipsies taking her sister away?

119

When Emma had finally dressed and wandered down to the sitting room she rather wished she had stayed in bed, for the tiny flat was crowded with pressmen. Reporters jostled photographers, and bulbs flashed as she walked into the room. Surprised and confused, she found herself answering questions, turning from one voice to another and blinking from the dazzle of flashlight after flashlight. Mark fared little better. The two were made to sit side by side on the settee, bulbs flashed again and the noise grew louder than ever.

'It isn't me you should be photographing,' Mark kept protesting. 'This gipsy lad, Eddy, is the one you want. He's down at Swallow Field. I tell you, if he hadn't risked his life by going down into the well, Emma wouldn't be here now. The rope wouldn't have held. All I did was pull them both up.'

He stood up to leave but found his way to the door barred by another eager questioner.

'You say he's a gipsy? Is he a friend of yours?'

Mark hesitated, remembering briefly the ugly scene in the shop a day or so earlier. 'No. We hardly know each other at all. Excuse me, but I've got a squash match to play, and I'm late already.'

Left alone to tell of the drama, Emma did what she could, mentioning Eddy's bravery but saying nothing of poor Elsie who had caused it all. Finally, she was rescued by her aunt who ushered her out of the room and into the peace and quiet of the back garden.

'You rest there now, I'll deal with the press.'

Emma sat down in the deckchair, watched her aunt bustling back to the house like a general marching into battle, and let her muscles relax a little. Her shoulders still hurt, though, and she winced as they came into contact with the wooden sides of the chair. Why didn't her aunt invest in something more modern, like the thickly-cushioned garden chairs that graced the patio at her home in Croydon?

She yawned, tilted her head to one side and saw Becky sauntering towards her from the house. If she had expected some warmth, a touch of sympathy perhaps, or even awe-struck excitement, then Emma was to be sorely disappointed.

'You are a silly ass.' Becky stood beside the chair, eyeing her cousin as a zoologist would eye some rare species of animal. 'What made you go to the cottage? Mary Ann warned of danger, she warned you. So why did you go?'

Emma opened her mouth in surprise, then shut it quickly as she searched about for a sensible answer. 'It seemed like a good idea at the time.'

'Then you want your brains testing! You could have been killed. Why didn't you heed Mary Ann?'

'Maybe because I didn't believe Mary Ann.'

Becky's eyes narrowed. 'She wouldn't lie.'

'I didn't mean that,' Emma said quickly. 'I only meant that I didn't believe she could see into the future.'

'But now you know better.' Becky smiled triumphantly. 'Now you know she really does have the power.'

'Oh come on, you make her sound like Merlin.' Emma shook her head in exasperation. 'Alright, so she sees pictures in the tea-leaves, but I still think it was only coincidence. I don't believe in seers, as you call them, any more than I believe in ghosts.' She paused, wondering why Becky always managed to get under her skin in this way. It made her want to hurt, when she should have been tactful.

'Think what you like.' Becky sat down on the lawn and started plucking out blades of grass in an absent manner. 'Anyway, you didn't tell me that you and Mark had been back to see her. Why not?'

Emma raised her eyebrows in surprise. 'Well, you were never around to tell, for one thing, and for another, I just didn't think it important.'

'Mark wouldn't have gone if he didn't think it important,' came the snappy retort.

Emma sighed and watched the sleek dark head bent to the task of destroying the lawn. So much for rest. Things were less tense in the sitting room, for all the noise and jostling.

'Anyway, how did you know we had been to Mary Ann's?'

'Mary Ann told me yesterday when she phoned.' Becky looked up at Emma. 'Oh yes, long before anyone else knew about the accident, Mary Ann was having premonitions. She said it first flashed through her mind at around four o'clock.'

'What did?'

'This picture of you, surrounded by darkness, and screaming.' Becky frowned. 'She said she had been getting it ever since you went to see her on Friday. She asked if you still had the stem of angelica.'

'Does she know now all that happened?'

Becky shrugged. 'It was only about five o'clock. We didn't know then. Still, I daresay someone has told her since. Now I suppose you're going to say that her premonition was just coincidence, too.'

Emma shook her head and was silent for a long time. Then at last she spoke.

'Perhaps some people pick up images, just as animals sense things.' She paused, remembering how Sheba had reacted to the cottage garden. But that had been a pigeon, surely? Certainly Elsie Hargreaves had been in the cottage, and probably hiding out in it for two weeks, but she could never have caused the bitch to be so frightened. No, it had to be the pigeon. 'Anyway, everything else proved to be perfectly logical – the books, I mean, coming from Elsie after all.'

Becky stared at her for a long time but said nothing as she attacked the grass again.

Sensing this was a good time to get away from her cousin, Emma got out of the chair and wandered slowly down the path, pretending to examine the flowers as she went. At the edge of the garden she stood, at peace with the world, staring out over the fields and hills, listening to the distant bleating of sheep and breathing in the smells of high summer.

She wondered when Mark would return to go with her to thank Eddy. It would have to wait now until after lunch, and that made her feel very guilty. After all, the gipsy lad *had* saved her life. She wanted to reward him, but Aunt Peggy thought that his proud parents might feel insulted at the gesture, even though it was kindly meant. Her eyes slid towards Swallow Field, then opened wide with disbelief.

'They've gone,' she cried aloud. 'The gipsies have gone!'

'Good riddance, then,' Becky had stopped attacking the grass and was now lying down with her hands behind her head. 'Funny though, they summer here every year, and don't leave until October as a rule. Funny.'

Funny? Emma felt bitter. No, it wasn't funny at all; it was tragic that Eddy was so afraid of being blamed, as his people were blamed once before, that the whole camp had packed up and left quietly in the night.

'Where have they gone?'

'I don't know.'

Emma turned swiftly. 'But we must find them. They can't be allowed to leave like this.'

'What?' Becky raised her head and stared at her cousin. 'You must be mad.'

'But how am I going to thank Eddy now?' Emma turned to look back at Swallow Field through eyes that were blurred with tears. Cows were grazing where, only yesterday, caravans had stood. Already it seemed that Eddy and his people had never been there at all.

A distant voice broke into her thoughts, her aunt's voice calling from the sitting room window.

'Emma! It's your father telephoning you. Hurry up, dear.'

Emma felt her heart turn over. Why was her father ringing at this time of day? The doctors had said that her mother was doing so well. Why, then, was her father ringing now?

Feeling a cold dread, she rushed into the house, up the stairs and entered the sitting room breathlessly. Everyone else had gone now, and her aunt was standing there alone, looking serious, with the phone in her hand.

'I haven't told him about the accident just yet,' she whispered.

Emma took the phone from her aunt, certain now that it was bad news. 'It's me, Dad. How's . . . how is . . .'

Her voice cracked, and she sank to the chair beside the small table. Then she heard her father speak and let her hunched shoulders fall with immense relief.

'What? She is? That's marvellous, Dad!' Emma gazed up at her aunt with shining eyes. 'Mum's coming out of hospital next week. She's well again, and there's nothing more to worry about. Dad's coming for me on Wednesday.'

She turned back to the phone and chatted happily to her father. 'What was that? Yes . . . yes, Dad. I've had a lovely time in Dorset.'

Aunt Peggy watched her brother put the suitcase into the back of the car, then hugged Emma tightly. 'Oh my dear, I *am* going to miss you. You'll come back to us again, won't you?'

'Otherwise life here will get very dull,' said Mark. 'No ghosts, no more daring-do's to rescue the fair maiden, no press reporters . . .'

'Oh hush up,' laughed Emma, feeling near to tears. She turned to Becky, unsure whether to kiss her or not. 'Well, goodbye. Take care now.'

Becky flashed a weak smile. 'Listen to who's talking.'

'You know what I mean,' whispered Emma. 'Take

a certain person with a pinch of salt, and remember that everything has a logical explanation.'

Becky said nothing to this, but pressed her cheek against Emma's lips. There was no warmth in her action, it was merely what was expected of her.

Emma got into the car, clipped on her seat-belt, then waved back at the little group standing outside Travis Groceries. As Mr Morris pressed his foot on to the accelerator, she twisted her head around to watch the receding figures of her aunt and cousins until they could be seen no more. Until this moment, she had not realized just how much she was going to miss them.

Mr Morris was chatting happily, conscious, no doubt, of her feelings, and desperately trying to pretend he had not spent sleepless nights after learning of the accident. But all that needed to be said had been said last night. He decided to let the subject drop, even though the thought of his daughter down the well sent shudders of horror through him.

Emma noticed he was driving across the Market Square and heading towards the lane. He had no choice in the one-way system around Athelbury, but she had hoped never to pass this way again.

They were in the lane now, and driving past the cricket field. 'I won't look,' Emma said to herself. 'I'll shut my eyes.' But as the car rounded the bend her gaze was drawn, like a magnet, to the old cottage. The first thing she saw was the hoarding that had been hastily erected around the well, with lettering painted on it in bold red paint:

DANGER KEEP OUT

Suddenly, her attention was drawn to the little boy standing on the kerbside by the green gate. He was waving a bunch of what might have passed for flowers at a distance but on closer inspection looked more like weeds.

'It's Tommy! Dad, can you pull in, please? He's waving us down.'

As the car drew to a halt, Emma opened the door and smiled at the little boy. He held out the mixture of weeds and wild flowers, staring at her solemnly.

'For me?' Delight mixing with surprise, Emma reached for the strange bouquet. 'That's very kind and thoughtful of you, Tommy. Thank you.'

'The lady asked me to pick them for you. She said "Pick roses for Emma." But they prickled, so I picked these instead.'

'Which lady?'

'The lady I saw the other day,' answered Tommy.

Emma frowned in puzzlement, but then her face cleared. 'Oh, you mean the one who sent you to get help?'

The fair head nodded vigorously. 'She said, "Pick roses for Emma and thank her for being so kind".'

Emma smiled. 'I see.' Her face clouded. 'No I don't. That lady has gone to Winchester.'

The little boy shook his head slowly from side to side. 'No. She's in her garden.'

Emma looked to where he pointed, and fell back into her seat as Tommy spoke again:

'She said, "Tell Emma, they're from the lady at ninety-nine".'